THE CAREGIVER

*To Donna,
My fellow Caregiver.
Hoping good things for
your future!
Lois Hauck*

THE CAREGIVER

❦

Lois T. Hauck

iUniverse, Inc.
New York Lincoln Shanghai

The Caregiver

All Rights Reserved © 2004 by Lois T. Hauck

No part of this book may be reproduced or transmitted in any form or by any means, graphic, electronic, or mechanical, including photocopying, recording, taping, or by any information storage retrieval system, without the written permission of the publisher.

iUniverse, Inc.

For information address:
iUniverse, Inc.
2021 Pine Lake Road, Suite 100
Lincoln, NE 68512
www.iuniverse.com

ISBN: 0-595-32145-3

Printed in the United States of America

CHAPTER 1

❀

All girls dream of the glamorous jobs they'll have when they grow up. What will I be? My thoughts spanned the horizon. A doctor? A missionary nurse in the wild bush of some third-world country? Maybe a researcher who will discover the cure for cancer. So, off I went to college, graduated, got married, and raised four children.... Oh, don't get me wrong. Being a wife and mother has its obvious rewards—but I still felt like a part of me was missing. Although I held a degree in education, I still felt that innate tug toward some people-helping career, at least loosely related to healthcare. What fed my soul the most was helping others. Maybe that's why I felt such total shock when all these good intentions seemed to crash.

I applied for a job doing home health care where I would be making rounds and providing various services for housebound people. This particular agency gave me my first list of patients and I was all set to start. New situations always made me apprehensive so I wasn't surprised to find how nervous I felt on that first day.

Driving north of town I found the tiny mobile home park where my first patient lived. I parked, walked up the steps to the front door, and after hesitating just for a brief second, knocked. Looking through the window of the door I saw an elderly man in his recliner chair. Without even looking up, he motioned with his hand for me to come on in.

Feeling awkward, especially with the silence that greeted me, I found myself wondering where to begin. My agency had been rather vague as to what my duties were going to be, but I guess I would eventually find out. Henrietta, his wife, was my patient and I assumed she was still in bed, which she was. The folder from the agency was on the counter and after looking through it I found that I was to help her with her personal hygiene, do the laundry, some cooking and also some cleaning.

The shower was a challenge because she was obese and could hardly walk. She had been in the hospital with pneumonia and was still so weak. I got her all cleaned up and in her chair then went to work on their lunch.

After tidying up a bit, it was soon time to leave so I drove to my next client's house on the east side of town. The neighborhood was upscale with tree-lined streets, well-manicured lawns and elegant older homes. I found the house, which was a large three story Tudor. The area was radically different than the previous neighborhood. I also wondered what this lady would be like. I had preconceived impressions because all the agency would tell me was that she suffered from depression and panic attacks. Wouldn't that have been enough information to turn my car around and head in the opposite direction? But I felt like I was ready to face a challenge today.

Basically, I figured, I was to be there as a companion although I had no idea how I would be able to help someone like that. This lady had even called the agency the day before, saying she didn't know what she would do if she started crying when I came.

I turned off my engine and nervously walked over to the porch. I finally got up enough nerve to ring the doorbell. Nothing happened so I was starting to think she wasn't at home. But after waiting a few moments, I could hear faint footsteps coming down the hall. The door creaked open and there she emerged, a short mousy lady with cropped stringy hair that looked like it hadn't been combed in a while. She seemed like she might be afraid of her own shadow.

After identifying myself, she asked me to come in. I curiously glanced around and could see that the rooms were elegantly furnished but since the blinds were drawn, the atmosphere was so cold and formal. No wonder she was suffering from depression.

We passed the spacious staircase and continuing down the hallway I followed her into the library. I would eventually end up spending many hours in this dreary room that she had turned into a bedroom for herself.

Mrs. Harvey, at this point, turned to me and said, "I hope you don't mind if I crawl back in bed. I am so tired and I haven't slept a wink in 2 ½ years."

I tried not to show my surprise and doubt to what must have been an exaggerated statement on her part, at the same time thinking, "What am I supposed to be doing while she is sleeping?"

She must have read my mind and stated, "I'm sorry I'm this tired. Since I never sleep, I am so weary that I can't keep my eyes open. Why don't we just talk while I have them shut."

We began to get acquainted this way with my asking questions about her family. This was more of a one-sided conversation but that was okay since the agency frowned on our revealing anything of a personal nature with our clients.

After a few basic "yes" and "no" answers, I discovered I must have opened a can of worms that related to her now deceased husband. When I had asked about him, her face puckered up in a frown and she sharply retorted, 'He was a bum!" All I had meant to find out was just his line of work, not a blunt description of his character!

He had been a dentist in the area and had had a mistress on the side for 25 years. She didn't suspect anything for the longest time, even when he had to work late almost every night. But one day she discovered some "love letters" that went into great detail. She confronted him with her discovery but all he did was shrug her off saying now it was her problem to deal with. I tried to change the subject but then she went into an "organ" recital, telling of all her aches and pains.

She had classical music playing in the background so coupled with the dismal room and the drone of her voice, I found myself fighting sleep. Soon her thoughts trailed to other members of her family and she began a rundown listing all of their vises and mannerisms that bothered her.

After an hour of this, she finally paused, opened her eyes, and as if in surprise, said, "Jodie, I can't believe I told you all that!" Her "revelations" must have been therapeutic because now she felt good enough to get up and fix herself some lunch.

I followed her out in the kitchen where I saw her dog cowering in the corner. I was thinking to myself, "I have heard of dogs that they say act like their owners, but this one actually looks like Mrs. Harvey!" The dog had gray stringy hair in her eyes and it was parted in the middle, just like hers. She seemed terrified of everything and tried to stay out of our way. Good thing that dogs didn't talk!

One day the crew who was responsible for taking care of her yard work arrived to find out what her latest complaint was. She had frantically called to say that they were urgently needed to come out right away and correct their error. Not knowing what they had done, they reluctantly rang her doorbell. She led all of us around to the back of the house and showed them a tiny stray weed that had cropped up behind a rock near her fountain area.

I have to hand it to one of the men. Instead of getting all defensive and upset at her outrageous expectation, he quietly replied, "Mrs. Harvey, you don't need a well manicured lawn. What you need is artificial grass."

I wanted to pat him on the back for his discerning statement, but I guess after all the years that he had tried to please her, he was finally seeing that his endeavors were impossible.

The days went into weeks and I was starting to get accustomed to the routine, although each day seemed to be different enough to be interesting, especially with other patients given to me here and there.

One day in early November, the agency called saying they needed me to fill in for Sally since she had hurt her back and couldn't take this next patient. All they told me was his name and address and that the assignment was for only an hour every morning. That was unusual since most of my patients needed me for only one or two days a week.

I rushed to get ready earlier that morning, knowing I needed to squeeze him in my schedule. After I got the children off to school I quickly jumped in the car to begin my rounds. I wasn't too thrilled to find out that this new patient lived in a high rise downtown, realizing that it would be a challenge finding a place to park. But the inconvenience would be temporary since I was just "filling in" and I was eager to get it over with.

I found a place to park in the garage beneath the building, then walked to the entrance of the apartments. This high rise was 32 stories tall with a hotel on the first seven, apartments on the next seven and condos on the upper floors. I was so happy to run into the cleaning lady, who happened to know Houston, my client, and she was able to show me where his apartment was. The hallways were a labyrinth and I'm sure I would have had trouble finding it by myself so I appreciated her willingness to help me out.

I'll never forget that first day, and I certainly never dreamed how this event marked the beginning of an important era in my life. I continued down the hallway with Darlene and she pointed out his apartment door. I knocked. No one answered. I knocked again. Again there was no answer. I slowly opened the door and peered in. I didn't see anyone so I cautiously stepped into the spacious living room, quickly glanced around and saw that it was sparsely furnished, then continued to walk in the bedroom. There he was—an extremely thin older man lying on his side with his head propped up on one hand. He was a partial quadraplegic so that explained why he had been unable to answer the door. At the same time I was thinking with concern, "My agency really needs to have better communication with me." On the other hand, if I had known he was paralyzed I probably would have declined the job, thinking that it was more than I could handle.

His back was towards me so I walked around the bed to face a scrawny man with a slightly balding head. Immediately his face lit up and he expressed enthusiastically, "Why…you're beautiful!"

I blushed thinking I was hearing a compliment, which it probably was but it wasn't long before I found out he told every woman that! Also, I didn't know until later that he was legally blind!

I was a little skeptical as to how I was to help him but he was very patient and was able to explain how his morning routine went. He verbally detailed step by step the instructions for the dressings on his pressure sores. These were areas that were frequently affected from lying in the same position hours upon hours. Amazingly, he received no other help except when a man came in the evening to put him to bed.

After finishing his personal hygiene, he very patiently explained how I was to get him up and into his chair. I wasn't very good at lifting and that would have been my main reason for not wanting to help with a quadrapalegic. I certainly hoped I wouldn't drop him!

We attempted what seemed to be the impossible and my endeavors were rewarded to see him safely seated on his scooter. Fortunately, he did have use of his left arm so he was able to hold on and steer with that one. But to keep his legs from flopping in the floor, I had to tie them together with a strap.

During that hour, I became more and more impressed with his positive attitude towards life in general. He told me he had Multiple Sclorosis and as time went by it gradually got worse over a 30-year period. The stress must have been too much for his wife of 25 years. She threw him out with only a few items of old furniture and he had to find a place to live by himself. Houston must have seen my look of consternation on my face because he immediately stated with concern, "Oh, don't look so sad. My wife actually did a favor for both of us when she did that!"

He was working for the Department of Natural Resources at that time but his eyesight was really failing from the disease. It wasn't long before he was forced into early retirement. He had found this spacious place to live and actually it was very convenient for him with the connecting skywalks to the bank, restaurants, and stores.

My hour with Houston passed quickly and I was actually dismayed to find out it was time to go. I could see that he needed so much more care than I had time to give. Frustration set in as I prepared myself to depart. His apartment really could have used some tidying up along with his needing to have a home cooked meal. But the short time I spent with him would be all the help he got each day with the exception of that from an older man who came in the evening for approximately ten minutes.

I was haunted by the whole experience. Later that evening when Steve came home from work I shared with him how this man had the most uplifting outlook on life when he could have used his condition for self-pity. He was amazed to hear the story so we both seemed glad when I got a call from my agency the next day saying Sally wouldn't be back and I was needed on a permanent basis. I was to help this man every morning before I looked after my other clients. This began a long and interesting assignment.

I don't mean to imply that Houston didn't have any rough edges. Those he certainly had. He had some choice words to say about those he didn't like plus he spent a lot of time alone with his bottle of Scotch. He had a witty yet worldly kind of personality so it soon became obvious that one of his favorite past times was trying to embarrass me when we were in public. Of course he found out right away that this wasn't hard to do. What a tease!

CHAPTER 2

❦

One day I had a little extra time to spend with Houston so I convinced him that I needed to wash his hair. Fussing and fuming, he kept protesting as I led the way into the kitchen. I gathered up his shampoo and towels then got his scooter into position by the sink. I had learned early on that he only pretended to be upset but on the inside really appreciated everything I did for him.

I had him back his chair up to the sink and after putting the towel around his neck, instructed him to lean back as I was getting the water ready. Suddenly he exclaimed, "Ouch, you're hurting me! The water is too hot!"

"Now wait a minute," I said with playful impatience, "I haven't even sprayed any water on you yet!" The mischievous smirk was on his face as he knew, then, that I had caught on to his antics.

"Houston!" I exclaimed, "I think the only way you feel exhilarated is when you are sneering and obstinate!"

He seemed amused at my glimpse into his playful but defiant character. There became many other times where it seemed he was finding it difficult to suppress secret laughter. At the same time I enjoyed returning his quips.

We had a nice conversation as I was scrubbing his head. He didn't have much hair but what was there, really needed some extra attention. He mentioned, "You talk as if you have been well educated."

I replied, "I wouldn't exactly say, 'well educated' but I did go to college and received my degree in education." I went on to say that I wanted to be more of a help to people on a one-to-one basis.

He was starting to let down his guard and said in a longing voice, "Maybe some day when you have a little extra time, we can go downstairs to the café and have some coffee. Do you drink coffee?"

"Yes," I answered and continued with a smile, "I would love to be able to do that with you."

I had some private cases on Tuesdays and Thursdays so it wasn't long before we got in a routine of going down for coffee before I went to these other cases. I had rearranged with these clients to go a bit later.

On the way down to the café, people stopped to chat with us and soon I realized what a social person Houston really was. Because of his being cooped up in his apartment for several years, he was longing to get out and mingle with others.

Stephanie, the café hostess soon made good friends with us and always tried to seat us where it was easy to get his scooter in and out. Soon it became obvious that the waitresses fought over who would wait on us. They enjoyed being teased by him along with witnessing his positive spirit.

One day we arrived for our morning coffee, and knowing that we usually came around 9AM, Stu, one of the waiters, had a table ready for us with name cards placed where we were to be seated. That was just one way the café staff made Houston feel like he was special. Of course they knew he would entertain them by having something funny to say such as, "My ex-wife tried to give me a gift certificate from Jack Kavorkian for Christmas but I wouldn't take it!"

He had told me stories about his ex-wife, Noreen. I was sure he had been exaggerating because I couldn't imagine anyone being that bazaar. "She's a nutcase!" he would say. After they had been married many years they had a two-story home built in a quiet suburb. Houston tried to keep peace by staying out of her way so he basically lived on the lower level and tried to be as independent as he could. He didn't have his paralysis yet but was already using a scooter chair for the weakness and tremors he was experiencing.

One day Noreen flipped out from reality and began throwing some of their furniture from the house off the balcony. She continued with her tyrade with expletives gushing from her mouth and eventually wound up in the psychotherapist's office. He uncovered some "repressed" memories that all of a sudden told her that she had been abused as a child. His "psycho-babble" made her realize, very soon after that, that she needed to "divorce" her parents, change her name to Liza and become a psychotherapist herself since this one had "helped" her so much. Going back to school was necessary to get the required courses for this new profession.

At the same time she didn't want to remain married to Houston because she had developed some other interest in a lady friend and it was at this point that she asked him to leave. He was hurt, of course, but wanted to depart without causing too many waves. Besides, she had been chiseling away at his self-dignity for several years now. "Her temperament was like a detonator!" He explained to me with obvious relief that he now has escaped.

She got everything. He gave her the house and whatever furniture she hadn't broken in her tyrade. That explained why his apartment was so sparsely furnished. He had some shabby hand-me-downs for furniture but no pictures and hardly any kitchen supplies. The walls were totally bare.

I had heard that he had a son named Bruce who was in his 30's and a daughter named Elinor, in her latter 20's. I always wondered why I never saw them come around. I also noticed that he hardly ever mentioned them without seeming agitated, especially with the mention of Bruce. I didn't feel that it was my place to ask why and just waited until he felt ready to talk about it.

One day I had a cancellation with Mrs. Harvey, who had gone to visit her daughter in California, so I had a little extra time to spend with Houston. He seemed delighted that I suggested we go for a "walk" outside. Knowing that our days were numbered as to when we would have nice enough weather to permit this, I was glad that we could get some fresh air.

We made our way down the elevator, stopping to speak to people that we knew along the way. Then we went out the front door and down the handicapped ramp to the sidewalk leading to the path alongside of the river. Soon this would become our favorite spot. We especially loved going out to the pedestrian bridge and stopping at the benches in the middle. I liked to sit down on one of them and we both watched the water rolling over the rocks below while we drank in the sunshine.

On this day, Houston must have felt like it was time to explain his animosity towards his son so he began by quietly saying, "I will never forgive Bruce for what he did to me."

I was daydreaming but this statement aroused me with a start!

"What did he do?" I asked in surprise.

"He took me to court and sued me for Power of Attorney!"

"How could he do that without your consent?" I felt amazed and angry!

"With his mother's help," he sighed and continued, "they were able to convince the judge that I was incompetent."

Knowing full well how competent and even brilliant Houston was, my heart went out to him to have been dealt this low blow from his own son. But at the same time I couldn't understand how they were able to accomplish this so easily.

As if reading my thoughts, Houston continued, "Yes, as it turned out my 'ex' who is a very powerful woman in the community, had some 'pull' with this judge so there you have it."

I was silent for a moment, not knowing what to say. I was a peacemaker by nature and thought that it might help to say something like, "Maybe he thought he could help you in this way." Of course I found out later that this wasn't the case.

"What kind of a relationship does your children have with their mother?" I candidly asked.

"They are intimidated with her and do what she says."

He continued but not without some sarcasm, "She has a very controlling personality and thinks she's the center of the universe."

I was to meet this son not too long after his dad's confession. He had been ordered by the judge to bring his father an allowance of $100 every Friday. He came by one day when I was there so I had a chance to meet him. I had already been told that he was a local disc jockey for a rock station and that he had hair down to his waist in a ponytail. Houston had paid for his son's education but he had wasted some of his credit hours by taking "filler" courses such as "How to Play Pool." Houston told me that bit of news with a sneer! I tried to overlook statements like that along with how he described his son as having an "elastic morality."

Our meeting passed without being too awkward and I seemed to think he was quiet and pleasant. He stayed for a few minutes, just long enough to put the allocated money in his dad's wallet that he kept in his wheelchair pouch. There weren't many words that passed between the two of them. Maybe it was because they didn't have much in common.

Now Elinor was a different matter. Every time her name was mentioned he would roll his eyes and sigh. She, being Native American, had been adopted as a child and they had had a time raising her. Every once in awhile I came in to Houston's room and found his phone lying by his pillow. When he rolled his eyes I knew that Elinor was on the phone. Twenty to thirty minutes later he picked the phone up and she was still talking, not even aware of what her dad had done.

I also became aware that most of his $100 disappeared much quicker than it should have each week. As fast as Bruce could get it to his dad, Elinor came over even faster to take as much of it as she could. Houston was aware of this but to "keep peace" let her take the money. These five-minute sessions were the only time he got to see her. Therefore he just put up with it. He would wistfully say, "Why can't I have a normal daughter?"

At the end of the week I decided to try and spruce up his place by bringing in things to hang on his bare walls using pictures that I no longer needed. He put up his usual fuss and rolled his eyes at me, but I could tell that he was pleased. I had discovered he loved Harleys and had even owned a few in the past. I was able to find some nice large posters and after framing them, hung them up.

The place was starting to look a little better when Christmas came around. I put a wreath on his wall and hung lights around the bookcase, along with some other decorations. Next, I broached the subject of buying gifts for his family. There went his eyes again. But I reminded him that his elderly parents, who were in their nineties, would appreciate hearing from him along with his sister and brother. They lived out of town and one even lived on the West Coast.

He amically agreed that he would like to send them something but balked at the idea of getting anything for Bruce and Elinor. Elinor had three children, or maybe I should say four. One she had given up for adoption but they had kept in contact with her through the years. I was pretty sure that Houston might want to get each of his grandchildren something, which he did.

I threw out some ideas and eventually we came up with a list. I looked forward to spending "other people's" money when I went to the store to get these gifts! And I also felt a little excitement in "cheating" Elinor out of her weekly "inheritance."

I thought he would enjoy hearing Christmas music so I brought a tape of various songs to play while I was wrapping some of the gifts. When I heard "The Little Drummer Boy," I laughingly told him that I was always transported back to my hometown in St. Albans, West Virginia whenever I would hear this song.

Mr. Caringer, my piano teacher had given me some carols to practice when I was in second grade and was just a beginner. My older sister had already been taking lessons for three years and was really into practicing. Not me. I was more interested with playing outside with my friends. But there was one chore that I hated worse than going over my exercises on the piano and that was doing dishes. Every evening after supper my sister was expected to wash dishes and I was to dry them. But I would jump up from the table and run to the piano to start practicing. Of course I was interrupted and ordered to do the dishes first, but at least I tried my best to get out of this chore.

I rode my bicycle to Mr. Caringer's house once a week and as I approached his ivy covered Tudor styled house, my heart started to beat rapidly with fear. This was anxiety not only due to the fact that he knew I hadn't spent the time I should have on my music but mainly because my imagination was running away with me. I was convinced that his house was haunted.

I coasted down the path leading to his house and slowed my bike to a stop just before the entrance. I put down the kickstand and swooping up my music books from the front basket in the process, with trepidation walked slowly up to the massive carved wooden door. The knocker that I could barely reach, echoed throughout the house. I can remember thinking, "I hope no one comes to the door. Then I can go home and play."

But no such luck!

After going for several lessons, my teacher told me to just open the door and wait for him in the front entryway, which I did from then on. But this entrance was scary in itself. I sat on an uncomfortable wooden bench and took in my surroundings. To my left were two steps leading down into the parlor—the room of torture for me, and probably more for him. In this parlor were two grand pianos. There was a lot of red. Thick red carpet, deep red velvet curtains with gold fringe clinging to the edges and several red table lamps with large prisms hanging down from each shade.

I could hear the ticking of his large grandfather clock while I waited, but listened more carefully for another sound that I really didn't want to hear. I had heard rumors that this piano teacher had a son who was crazy and lived in the attic. While I waited there on the bench, my gaze went to the foot of the winding staircase to my right. I was sure that these stairs must lead to the attic where the crazy person was kept, so at the slightest sound of them creaking, I jumped and my hands clamped down on the arm of the bench I was sitting on. Fortunately he never appeared but I was sure I heard movements and scuffling sounds coming from upstairs each time I was there.

I don't know what I would have done if he would have come into sight. But I had to go through this fearful time once a week for the next seven years!

But back to "The Little Drummer Boy." I was just a beginner, as I mentioned before, and somehow couldn't get the timing just right. Mr. Carringer was a stickler for timing, more so, I think than selecting the right notes. This one day he was eating a snack of crackers and some kind of pungent cheese. I must have really slaughtered the piece so he grabbed a ruler to rap out the beat on my knuckles and at the same time said with impatience, "No, it goes pa, rump, pa pa pum." With each "p" sound some of his smelly cheese and crackers were sprayed out on my hands. No wonder I don't care for that song today. But at the same time, he instilled in me the need for having correct timing when with what little musical ability I had finally kicked in.

Houston really enjoyed hearing this story and wanted to turn the song up full blast whenever it would come on. I, of course, wanted to skip over it.

I continued to work on him with the idea of getting something for Bruce and Elinor, too. Again he rolled his eyes and said they didn't deserve anything. Finally, I convinced him. So we brainstormed and came up with several ideas. I was pleased that at least he was trying to make an effort in rebuilding a relationship with his two children.

I was also assigned to a cute elderly couple living south of town. Arnie and Erma were in the early 80's and lived in a neat little ranch house. I immediately felt right at home the first time I walked in and knew that my time with them would be special.

Earlier Erma was involved in a car wreck that left her having to recuperate from a broken hip. Arnie had been trying to care for her but their family wanted him to get some respite so they contacted my agency to have someone come in a few days a week.

He reminded me of my Dad because he liked to keep busy and even for his age had many interests and abilities. I got to be with them three days a week, four hours each day so that gave me enough time to do a lot of cooking, physical therapy, laundry, personal care and errands.

This was their second marriage due to the death of their spouses and they both had grown children. Soon I was to get to know each one of them, along with the grandchildren and it was a real pleasure to spend those few hours with this delightful couple each week.

Christmas came and Houston kept trying to act nonchalant about the whole season. But it was obvious that this was a special Christmas. The stockings for the grandkids were full and the wrapped presents were arranged in neat piles around the living room. I wasn't there when his family came to open them but from the looks of the torn off wrapping paper when I arrived the next day, I could tell that they must have enjoyed themselves. It was only too bad that his parents weren't able to make it in for a visit, because of bad weather. They also needed to wait until his sister, Joan, was able to drive them since they lived several hours away and they hadn't driven themselves in years.

I found myself coming over to his apartment more and more. It seemed a perfect stopping place in between my other patients. I knew he certainly could use some extra help since no one else was there to do things for him.

He hadn't been eating right so I began "fussing" over him and saying he needed to gain some weight. I began by bringing him prepared food from home, usually leftovers that my family hadn't eaten, and he seemed to really enjoy a change from his bachelor food of peanut butter and Spam.

Every once in awhile Jordan, our youngest son who was eight at the time, accompanied me on my visit with Houston and they both seemed to look forward to these visits. They began discussing subjects such as rare coins or geographic locations where they both had visited and before we knew it, we had to get ready to go. About the only time I had to tidy up the place was during these visits because Houston never wanted me to do domestic chores, knowing the time used in doing those would take the place of our "coffee time" or "walk time." He made excuses along the lines of, "It'll keep," or "save it for Elinor when she comes for her money."

Another reason Jordan liked to go with me was his desire to see one of our security guard friends. Boris was a large jovial fellow with a heavy Russian accent. We sometimes bumped into him when he was making his rounds and he always had something comical to say. Jordan thought it was funny when Boris lowered his eyes and said to me in somewhat of a stern voice, "Vut eze the goot for nothing Amedican voman doing?" He always made over Houston in a big way and said things like he was sure Houston was being abused by me. That, of course, delighted my patient because he always joked about that very thing!

One day Boris said with some concern, "Goot for nothing Amedican voman needs to be home weeth family." I guess he had noticed how often I came to help Houston.

I took him by the collar (and he was over twice as big as I was), and half jokingly, half seriously, said, "Listen, Buster, my family isn't neglected. I am home every day by the time the kids get off from school, plus every evening they get a home cooked meal."

I knew that the last comment would go straight to his heart, which it did so quickly he stated, "Scuze me, scuze me. Home cooked meal?? Vedy goot of Amedican voman." And he never again mentioned about my family being slighted!

Houston had two dependable friends, Skip and Martha. They were friends he used to work with in the past and they came to visit him on separate occasions. He perked up during their visits and thoroughly enjoyed these times of being about to reminisce. Sometimes Martha came at lunchtime and the two of them went downstairs to get a bite to eat. I was thankful for these two wonderful people. It wasn't very convenient for visitors to come, mainly due to the parking conditions, but they still made an effort to visit faithfully.

CHAPTER 3

I had a secret. Houston was going to be 59 in a few weeks and I wanted to do something special for him. He looked a lot older than 59, due to his poor health, but he certainly acted younger. I had made him a birthday cake and on the sly invited some of his friends to come up to his apartment that afternoon. I arrived a little earlier than usual that morning so I could quietly decorate his dining room without him knowing I was there. His doorknob had the tendency to squeak when I opened the door, but I found if I turned it slowly I could enter without him knowing.

I unfolded a freshly pressed tablecloth and arranged it neatly on his dining room table. Next I opened a large bag I had brought from home, emptying out the decorations to hang. After the crepe paper, banner and balloons were up, I stepped back to observe how the room looked. I wasn't sure if he would even notice since he spent the morning and part of the afternoon in the living room in front of his TV. But of course, where did he go first when he got on his scooter?—the dining room!

"What's this?" he asked in an amazed voice. Then he pretended to be upset with me for remembering his birthday.

There were two cakes on the table, coffee in a thermal carafe, some mints and nuts in a bowl and punch in a pitcher. I used the excuse that I had placed these on the table in case people stopped in while I was gone and they would want to help him celebrate. Again the eyes rolled. I gave him a quick hug then I was off to visit Mr. Edmore, one of my new clients.

I had invited Bruce and Elinor but they didn't seem to think they could make it. Typical. But maybe they would come the next day. Besides, the next day was Friday when Bruce brought his dad some money and Elinor came to get her share.

I came back in the afternoon and Houston was all ready to go for his walk. I hastily said, "Not now. We need to wait just a bit in case you have some visitors."

"Visitors…I'm not expecting any visitors!" he said with a growl.

The words barely escaped his lips when there was a knock on the door and in walked Skip. Following Skip was Stephanie, the hostess from the café downstairs, and behind her was Sally and Carmen, the two managers of the building along with Ben the hotel's interior decorator. Jamail, a neighbor and a fireman by trade, made his appearance. We laughed as he put on a party hat because it looked so tiny on his massive build. Everyone else put on party hats and helped themselves to the cake, punch and coffee.

Several neighbors joined us including a man I dubbed "Pastor Ray." Pastor Ray was a tall energetic man with flowing white hair. He helped out hurting churches, mainly those without pastors and he was involved in several other ministries in the downtown area. He related to everyone he met and was so easy to talk with.

I was sorry not to have invited Martha. I didn't know her last name nor know how to reach her. She later forgave me for not including her on the party list.

Houston never smiled, but when I looked at his face I could see he was happy. He was drinking in every word that people were saying to him. He even had two pieces of cake. By the time the last person left, I knew he would be exhausted so I offered to put him back into bed. The man coming to do this wouldn't be there for another hour or two so he took me up on my offer. I had to learn a new routine in getting him in bed. It certainly seemed easier than getting him up but still involved a lot of lifting and adjusting. I laid out his pills on his radio so that they were within reach. He had me arrange them on top so that he could get what he wanted whenever he needed to. So having done most of his evening procedure, I smiled at him then told him I'd be back the following morning.

Days and even months later, he kept referring to his party. He couldn't get over all the people who came. "Yes," I said with a smile, "I had to bribe them into coming."

"Oh, you…," he responded with a smirk. He told his parents when they called and they were pleased that he had had such a good time. I spoke with them briefly on the phone and they sounded delightful. I was really looking forward to meeting them.

On April Fool's Day I had talked Houston into playing a trick on Bruce. I had purchased a fake earring that was magnetic and made sure Houston was wearing it that afternoon when his son was scheduled to bring his dad his weekly allowance. He didn't exactly fall for our joke but a big smile spread across his face as his admitted, "Now that is funny."

Mr. Edmore, my newest patient, was almost indescribable. He lived in a run-down housing district with his apartment being on the third floor. The creaky elevator took me up to his place and my eyes gradually got used to the dimness of the dank hallway as I made my way to his dwelling.

His tall lanky form leaned on his specially made crutches as he used one to prop open the door to let me in. It never ceased to amaze me how he could predict exactly when I was to arrive but I later discovered he had a "security channel" on his TV that showed people coming in and out of the front door downstairs. He watched this particular channel hours upon end.

His rooms were practically bare but one item stood out from the rest and that was his large draftsman's table. He had been an architect in his prime and his artistic abilities were still put to use in several drawings in the makings on his table. Later I discovered his nickname was "The Master of Disaster" because of his many renderings of shipwrecks. He had perfected the technique of "angry" waves and no one else had even come close to knowing his method, which he claimed he would "take to his grave."

But there were no drawings of his to be seen on his apartment walls. He had given most of them away and the rest were stashed away in an old tattered portfolio in the corner.

His eccentricity was seen further when he gave me orders to wash his paper plates and plastic forks before I threw them away. One day he had me searching for an old razor. He claimed he hadn't seen it for a month but knew it was around. I figured I could find it right away since he only had three small rooms. I opened all the drawers, looked in cabinets, closets, baskets, and other areas. Finally he said, "Jodie, did you look in my toolbox?"

I had no idea why he thought I would have looked there, but to please him that's where I looked next. The top section had old tools laid out on the tray. I lifted up the upper half and underneath discovered a set mouse trap. Unbelievably, underneath the trap was the tiny box holding his razor!

"Why did you put it there?" I asked with amazement, trying hard not to laugh.

"In case someone broke in here and tried to rob me!" he replied seriously.

He had three alarm clocks that he set each night and they were all placed strategically near the head of his bed. I questioned why he needed that many and he answered, "In case one doesn't work." Of course I was amused, knowing there really wasn't an urgency to his wakening schedule.

Houston and I were going for a walk but this time indoors since the weather was much too cold to go out. We were hoping to run into some of our friends that had been to the party so we parked ourselves down on 2nd floor in the main lobby of the building. I was getting in the habit of bringing the newspaper from home to get him caught up on current events. I also had our neighborhood paper that came weekly. A favorite column of ours ran in this paper. Some rich philanthropist had found ways of giving away his money to people and the ones chosen were those who composed the most interesting letters to him.

There were the ones of young struggling couples trying to make ends meet, or maybe someone wanted to take his wife out for an anniversary but couldn't afford enough to make the event memorable. Sometimes the request was "off the charts" but it was worth reading to hear Houston's sarcastic comments. Invariably I ended up laughing, more at him than the ridiculous petition.

So many times, during these afternoons, different people in the building came up to me and asked, "Why don't his kids ever come to visit?"

Their comments put me in an awkward position but I always tried to say something such as, "They grew up with their dad being sick and maybe now they just need to live their own lives." Or I sometimes stated, "They are very busy." I don't know why I defended them. But it didn't escape his neighbors notice that his own family had abandoned him.

One day, one of the articles I was reading him caused me to laugh so hard I could hardly finish. This was something that had happened just the day before and somehow we missed it!

As I had mentioned before, one of our favorite places to go was on the blue pedestrian bridge outside of his building. We liked to look below at the water rushing over the rocks. There was one huge rock that stuck out from the rest and that's where this story took place. Apparently some deranged man was out there on the rock without any clothes on!

Remembering how cold it was, probably in the low 40's, I just couldn't believe it! People were stopping on the bridge to look over and see what was going on. Even those from a nearby museum were looking out of the big glassed in area by the river.

The fire department had been called and they were trying to reach this man by boat but got hung up in the shallow part of the river. They were forced to use their waders and try to reach him by foot. Several policemen were on the embankment trying not to laugh, but at the same time were glad they weren't the ones who had to try and rescue this person. Finally the firemen reached him but he began flaying with his arms to make them keep their distance. When they asked what he thought he was doing he belligerently replied, "I'm practicing to be a Navy Seal!"

I later found out he was taken to a local mental facility for evaluation.

I could tell that Houston was trying to control his mirth. Stories like this were ones he liked the most but of course never laughed at out loud.

I brought stories from home, mentioning to Houston antics my kids were up to or things that they said. He always was so interested in everyone and loved to hear what each were up to. I made him suffer through the endless cat stories. Holly was always rescuing animals and would bring them home to nurse back to health. We had lived in Grand Rapids for five years but before she even consented to move with us, we had to promise that we would dig up Muffin in our back yard and rebury her once we got here!

Several people were helping us unload the truck when one of them picked up a big black garbage bag with a twisty on it.

"What this?" he asked with curiosity.

"Why it's Muffin, our dead cat," I replied nonchalantly.

With that he quickly dropped the bag and looked at me like I was crazy. Apparently he didn't have a 14 year old daughter. Houston enjoyed hearing stories such as this one, even if it had to do with cats.

Every once in awhile I came in his room and he knew that something was wrong because I was rather subdued. Of course I got teased since he accused me of talking his leg off. I don't think he had been a sensitive man before his illness, but what he had gone through in the past years had given him certain abilities of perception.

The weather finally cleared up enough for his parents to come for a visit. Houston's sister Joan and her husband Tom drove them and also brought lunch. I came by after my last client and was finally able to meet his family. I found them to be really sweet, especially his mother and dad. They were remarkably spry for being in their 90's and were as sharp as a tack. I could see where he got his brilliant mind.

His dad had been a test pilot in the 1940's and I enjoyed hearing some of his stories. One could imagine Houston's mother bustling about in the kitchen with her little apron on. Joan and Tom were also very nice. Joan had my attention when she started telling about some of her troubled students that she taught in an alternative school. My husband had done the same for only one year and that year had seemed like ten.

Soon their visit came to an end. They were anxious about getting out of town before another snowstorm hit. I could see that Houston was tired out so again offered to put him to bed. He took me up on it, while at the same time fussed, moaned and grunted while I was helping get him ready. Before I left, he quietly thanked me. His comment was barely audible, almost as if he didn't want me to hear. I left his apartment with a smile and a feeling of satisfaction.

Some days when I returned, I found him slumped down in his scooter chair with his head hanging over the side. I was becoming more and more alarmed with the danger of his situation, especially since he was alone throughout most of the day. He confessed that one day, before I started working for him, he had driven his scooter over to the kitchen to get something out of the refrigerator. He reached for it, lost his balance, and there he was, in the refrigerator for the entire day until Sam, the man who put him to bed in the evening, arrived. I certainly didn't like hearing that story and made him promise to tell his son.

Eventually the time was arranged for him to be fitted for a custom made computerized wheelchair. We had about an 8-month wait since the physical therapist had to take body measurements plus check for his pressure points so that he would get a better fit in the chair. The seat and back cushions were specially designed by NASA. They not only regulated air flowing through them but also redistributed his weight every few minutes so that new pressure sores wouldn't be started. This was good news to me because the treatments I was giving him for his open wounds were constantly having to be reevaluated and changed.

I had been taking him every other week to the Wound Care Center and had been following their orders. His sores would start to get better, and some would even completely heal, but then others would open up.

Of course this was mainly caused by my not being able to change his position every hour.

The medical staff at the Wound Care Center told me that his M.S. was also a big factor in interfering with the healing process. Some treatments that would work some weeks would stop working the next week. But at the same time the staff kept complementing me on my persistent care saying his health was much better since I had come on board.

So I was always having to learn new procedures. I enjoyed the challenge. The doctor commended me on how fast I caught on and even said he could tell that Houston was in good hands. That would be when I had to give Houston a light punch for rolling his eyes.

One day the doctor even allowed me to assist in doing a surgical procedure he had to do with the wounds, saying that he trusted me as much as his own nurses. That really made my day.

Finally the day came for the wheelchair to be delivered. I was so thrilled because it was becoming more and more evident that Houston was having increased difficulty staying upright on his scooter. This chair not only had supports all around him but also had a joystick that he could control and maneuver wherever he wanted to go. A delightful added feature was that the chair could totally recline to not only enable him to have a nap but also relieve some of the pressure.

After hearing the cost, I was sure it would have come with a TV and VCR, too! One thing we hadn't counted on, though, was that it would take several months to get used to the steering. There were more gouged holes in his wall than I could count.

One evening I brought Todd, my oldest son, to not only meet him but also to help repair some of these holes. I didn't want to bother Ben, the resident painter who had more than his share of work to do for the building. Todd was handy with spackle and we were pleased with the finished product. Ben came the next day and touched up the paint job, then gave us a small container and brush to do this ourselves the next time we needed to (which was often!).

The other new responsibility that I had to get used to was taking the motorized wheelchair apart and putting it back together. Parts had to get detached in order to get close enough to the bed to do the transfer. Then when I got him in the chair, the parts had to be reattached. I had to guide it over against the wall and plug it in to get recharged. I couldn't tease him about his steering ability after experiencing firsthand how sensitive it was to even a small touch.

The chair's assembly seemed so complicated and had a mind of it's own, but after doing the same thing for several months, I finally could practically take it apart and put it back together blindfolded. The people at the Wound Care Clinic were always amazed as to how fast I could do this feat!

My agency called and told me to go to a new patients house the next morning after I got done with Houston. I was to be with this lady twice a week for two hours each time. Houston teased me ahead of time saying, "Are you sure she will be able to take all of your abuse?" He thought his morning bath and shave was all the maltreatment he could take.

🍁   🍁   🍁

The neighborhood was close to Mrs. Harvey's and also was an older but elegant one. I had wondered what had become of Mrs. Harvey since she had come back from her daughters. I had been given other clients while she was gone but when she returned my agency told her I wasn't available anymore. That made her mad. I guess I should have taken her anger as a compliment. I was grateful for the break from her depressive situation. I don't think the agency ever got anyone to replace me since she was such a complainer.

The new patient, Mrs. McMann, was a tall, graceful and rather austere lady with white hair swept up on top of her high forehead. She immediately struck me as "The Baroness" on The Sound of Music. When walking in a room she commanded attention. Not much longer, after the first occasion of meeting her, I found out her nickname was "The Baroness!"

I would never have guessed that she was 92, but more like 75. Her now deceased husband had been an attorney and she had come into money when her parents died. They had owned a local business that had been prosperous. The house had been elegant at one time but had been neglected in the latter part of the 68 years she had lived there.

Mrs. McMann had the "better-than-thou" attitude with everyone she met. Maybe it was because she was President of the Literary Club, President of the Music Society and on the board of the Symphony along with one of the local hospitals. She had something unkind to say about everyone, including her own family, but for some reason we got along fine.

But the truth of the matter was I always got a knot in my stomach right before I was to arrive at her house, thinking that this was the day that she would turn on me. Also, I didn't relish having to do some of the outlandish chores she assigned to me each day.

I never was sure what she had in mind for me to do each day that I went but invariably I had to endure the wrath she poured out against her son, J.T. They both seemed to be strong-willed and neither would give in on many different issues. One in particular was that he wanted her in a home and she wouldn't hear of it. "Over my dead body!" she constantly said.

After getting acquainted a bit she had me do an unusual task of moth proofing her "woolens." I had no idea how to do this especially since I detested the smell of mothballs, so I told her she would need to instruct me what to do. She seemed surprised and asked, "Then what do you do with your woolens?"

I just said we didn't have moths. I could have said we didn't have woolens either but didn't want her to die of a heart attack right there on the spot!

She had me take these "woolens" outside and brush them with a special brush. I didn't have the foggiest clue what I was brushing them for but did as I was told. Then I had to spray them with some smelly old moth spray. I got the task finished but felt like I reeked of mothballs the rest of the day.

Next she had me clean out her medicine cabinet. She asked, "How long are you supposed to keep medicine?"

"One year," I answered.

"Oh," she said, "I have some that are a little older than that. Do you think they are still good?"

After looking at the dates, I thought that 40-50 years old exceeded the "little old" mark, so tossed them in the garbage. These had even started to decompose.

Another chore she had me do was to get out her good silver and polish it. I felt like this was such a waste of time knowing she was never going to entertain. Also, there was no one who would want to come over to put up with her abuse since she badmouthed everyone. Still the two of us continued to get along.

One day I arrived at her house only to find her on the front porch pacing back and forth. She seemed irritated that I was late, although according to my watch I wasn't at all. Surprisingly, she had on her good Sunday dress, a pillbox hat, and little white gloves.

Her macramé purse was hanging from her wrist.

I started to get out of the car but she demanded that I stay in and follow her. Follow her where?…I didn't know. She had absolutely refused to ride with me up until this point, reminding me of the lady who starred in the movie "Driving Miss Daisy."

She climbed into her old blue Mercury and we both backed out of the driveway together. Only by the time she put hers in drive, I wasn't able to catch up to her! She whizzed down the street, through stop signs and had turned the corner before I could figure out where to go. I had to go faster than I should have, being afraid of losing her.

As we came to the busiest street in that part of town where three streets come together, I looked in horror as she continued right on through the red light, but then her car stalled in the center of this intersection. Amazingly enough, no one honked at her.

She tried restarting it, but her car just whined. That quickly, she hopped out then proceeded to the back of her car and tried to give it a little push! I know that those looking couldn't believe their eyes to see a little old lady with a pillbox hat, white gloves and macramé purse (which was still dangling from around her wrist) trying to push her car!

Her car, of course, didn't budge. I couldn't let her stay in the busy intersection possibly getting hit, so I was forced to get out of my car and go over to see if I could convince her to get in with me. As I approached her I asked what she was doing and her reply was, "I'm trying to encourage this {expletive} car along."

Still she wouldn't come with me so I had her get back in her car and try to get it started again.

After two tries the engine finally turned over but the car was barely able to chug through the intersection. I didn't care. I was just glad to get out of that predicament. I slowly continued to follow her and discovered she was taking the car in to get it serviced. She hadn't planned on coming back with me but they couldn't find out what was wrong with her car that day so she was forced to drive home with me. She reluctantly gave in and that was the beginning of her being transported with me.

The days when we went grocery shopping were an adventure in itself. She didn't like it but since her car was still in the shop she was having to get used to the idea of riding with me. We pulled into the store parking lot where she tried to make me park in a handicapped spot. I refused so she started fussing and fuming. Mrs. Harvey had done the same thing with me. As a matter of fact, this was the same store she made me come to! What was it with these rich old ladies? They thought they were entitled to special privileges. Just then a feeling of apprehension came over me as I began to wonder if I would run into Mrs. Harvey while we were shopping! That's all I needed, to have two of them together!

Mrs. McMann continued to have a fit until I obeyed her and parked illegally. I told myself I would make her pay for the ticket if I got one. I had learned to pander to her wishes, thinking she wouldn't be as disagreeable if I did. She triumphantly got out of her side of the car and waited for me to come around to assist her. Adjusting one of her gloves, she lifted her head high in the air and followed me into the store.

I walked down each aisle with her while she pushed her cart with her white-gloved hands. After getting in line to check out she always had a fit if anyone were in front of her. But the most embarrassing time was when it was her turn and she insisted that they give her the prices from last week's ad since she wasn't able to come in then.

The store was used to her making absurd demands such as this one and I guess decided it was better to just give in rather than make a scene. Usually she got her discounted price or other ridiculous requests.

Another method she used was bullying the cashier into taking coupons even though she didn't buy the item. She claimed she bought the items the week before. Again they gave in. I always could see the clerks eyeing us, as we came in the store. I knew what they were thinking, "Oh, no! Please don't let her get in my lane!" She could probably have gone up to any of the checkers and said, "You didn't give me the correct change last week," and they would open up their drawers saying, "Here, take what you need!"

🍁　　　🍁　　　🍁

I was soaking Houston's hands in a bowl of soapy water to get his nails softer so I could clip them one afternoon. I said, "Houston, I am always so amazed as to how upbeat you are. Are you really that way on the inside, too?"

His answer startled me. He stated that the lowest point in his life was when his ex-wife and son Bruce had sued him for Power of Attorney. It was at that moment he thought about throwing himself out the window. This was the only time he had ever contemplated suicide, he said, but now he felt like he had something to live for. I was humbled by his admission! I had already been noticing that he was drinking less and less each day. It wasn't long before he stopped drinking all together.

Sally had been the girl I had replaced when she hurt her back. I knew she had only been with him for a couple of months and wondered who he had aiding him before that time. His daughter Elinor had just gotten a divorce and her ex-husband needed a place to stay for a while. That's when Randy moved in with him and became his helper. He assisted him all right. He helped himself to the money and ended up embezzling thousands of dollars from Houston! By the time this was discovered he had lost a lot of money so he asked Randy to leave immediately. He said that if he did he wouldn't prosecute.

I continued to bring food from home because I wanted to make sure Houston was eating right. It still amazed me how he could be left alone without any help from others. I didn't charge him for the meals but did let him pay me for some other items he had me purchase at the store. He was still fussing at me for throwing away his two-week-old French toast that had mold on it. I had done that the first week I went to work for him and he wasn't going to let me forget it!

"You old bachelor, you!" I teasingly said to him.

"You made me miss out on some good tasting food," he growled, "not to mention the fact that you wasted it!"

🍁   🍁   🍁

Mrs. McMann had another chore for me. She wanted me to vacuum her entire house. The only catch was that her vacuum was broken and she wanted me to use the dust buster! Well, that took up the whole two hours I was assigned to her. I'm sure I must have looked old and decrepit myself when I got done since I could barely straighten up. I must have looked like old Mrs. Hill who we lived next to when we first were married. She was an elderly neighbor who had an immaculate flower garden that she tended to every day. We never saw her face in the several years we lived next to her because she was always bent over weeding, hours upon hours, days upon days.

One day Steve borrowed a friend's rototiller to use in a garden we were starting. He had no idea how powerful the thing was until it was too late. After turning it on, it cut across our lawn and right through her prize-winning flowerbed! I'm sorry to say she passed away within the month. I heard she was taken with a sudden illness but we were always wondering if Steve's accident had brought it on!

So here I was, all doubled over like she was, doing Mrs. McMann's carpets. I was able to convince her she needed to get her original vacuum repaired so on the next visit we both took it to the repair shop. I should have expected what occurred there! She angrily scolded the repair man, saying her now deceased husband, "God bless his soul," had bought her that vacuum and he would be appalled it had only lasted 40 years! The man sheepishly looked at her then gave me a glance of sympathy. I'm sure he thought I was her daughter.

The same thing happened when we took her electric typewriter to get fixed. She was one of the few people who still used one and didn't know how obsolete they had become. The repairman seemed a little unsure he could get the part so out from her mouth came all the four letter words she could muster as she began telling him what she thought of his ignorance. I wanted out of there, fast!

I knew she was very "uppity" so it came as no surprise when she started criticising her daughter-in-law. She was telling me how one day she and her husband had given the family silverware to this daughter-in-law.

"And do you know what she did with it?" She asked me with a sniff, "She put it in the drawer with the everyday silverware! Father [meaning her husband] and I just sat there and cried!"

She went on to say, "You know, she's from Canada. She's not...'one of us'. She didn't even know what a bouillon spoon was and put it in the sugar bowl! Can you imagine?"

No, I couldn't imagine. I couldn't imagine what she would think if she looked in my silverware drawer at home and saw all the mismatched sets along with the spoons that had nicked places on the sides where they had accidentally fallen in the garbage disposer! Well that certainly would be my little secret.

CHAPTER 4

Soon the weather started to clear up. Houston and I were thrilled that we would be able to resume our walks outside. We had been thankful for the skywalk that connected to the whole downtown area and had discovered a little coffee shop run by a blind man and his wife. Charlie and Katherine loved to kid around and were a joy to be with. If we skipped a day, they were always concerned that something had happened to us.

The skywalk was great but it wasn't the same as being outside in the fresh air. Houston was anxious to sit in the sun while on the blue pedestrian bridge. He liked to see birds swoop down to rest on the big rock sticking out of the water. This was the famous rock of the "Navy Seal." I could never look at it without suppressing a chuckle!

My schedule was changing constantly with new patients I had to juggle around my regularly scheduled hours to fit everyone in. Eventually, Tuesdays became freed up during the lunch hour so we began going out to eat together at area restaurants. I tried to encourage Houston to invite Bruce to come along too, hoping that they would be able to patch up their fragmented relationship. One day he accepted our invitation and met us at the restaurant across the street. He worked close by so this was a good arrangement

Being together was awkward at first but soon Houston had the waitresses laughing at something he had said and then we all joined in. That broke the ice and we all felt more at ease after that.

On another occasion, Bruce brought his girlfriend Tonya along and the four of us had a great time. Tonya enjoyed hearing all of his escapades and she chuckled when she saw how he delighted in teasing me. Afterwards, they thanked me for all I had done for their dad and said he hadn't looked that good in years. I left there feeling really good.

🍁 🍁 🍁

Spring was definitely here. I had promised Houston a trip up north to see his sister and parents so I decided that now was the time to go. I was getting a little more used to driving his specially equipped handicapped van by now, and learned how to maneuver the ramp on the side.

I wasn't sure if Houston could hold up all day without a nap so was glad that his new wheelchair reclined. I encouraged him to rest during most of the trip, but instead he was trying to peek out to see things and make funny comments along the way.

The trip could have seemed long but hearing his remarks made the time go by quickly. The tiny towns that we went through certainly were interesting. One in particular was filled with many things to see. There was an old flea market with rusted items that must have been outside for years. It wasn't too hard to continue driving on by without stopping although usually my car pulled in automatically!

We even passed a trailer graveyard! I never saw so many trashed trailers in my life. I certainly would need to take a picture of this on the way back so that I would have some ammunition when my friends started taunting me about my home place in West Virginia.

Nearby was a racetrack for drag racing. Interestly enough this track was located right next to a propane tank business! I definitely didn't want to experience being around when one of the cars went astray!

Across the street was a lawn mower repair shop. Sitting out front were mowers for sale with prices ranging from $2.50 and up. What kind of a mower would be only $2.50?

That same town had a cute sign above a restaurant, "Dine with the Stars." This sign was shaped like a star and had famous Hollywood names on it like Bogart, Stewart, and Gable. I laughingly mentioned to Houston, "In a town this small, they must mean someone like Thelma Bogart, Oscar Stewart, and Edna Gable."

So much for that interesting little town. We passed many more and continued to enjoy seeing the freshness of new leaves on the trees and the farmers getting their gardens ready to plant.

I kept looking for barns to photograph. One of my hobbies was taking pictures of old ones and Houston was patient when I pulled off the road several times to get a good shot. The rustic unpainted structures were my favorite. Maybe it was because I spent many hours playing in similar ones as a child.

His parents were eagerly pacing the floors waiting for our arrival. The family had prepared a big dinner for our "lunch" and one could see how excited they were to have Houston there in person. His mother bustled around in the kitchen with her little apron on. The aroma filled the air with what she was preparing. His dad had me sit down to show me some family pictures. He was such a cute little man, very articulate and with a dry sense of humor. I could see where Houston inherited his wit. Some of the stories he told of his being a test pilot were breathtaking.

Houston's sister Joan and her husband Tom were also delighted to have their brother home. They were fussing over him to make sure he was comfortable. Tom was like Houston so it wasn't long before both of them started teasing me!

We enjoyed our big lunch/dinner, whatever you want to call it, then stayed for another hour or two before it was time to return home. We promised his parents that we would be back up but maybe next time they could come and visit us. They said they would do that soon, especially with the indication of summer around the corner.

My family was becoming more and more involved with Houston. I think they enjoyed hearing the friendly banter back and forth that we did to each other. Steve, my husband, came with me to take him to see the big Festival Parade that passed directly outside his building. Jordan came along too and was very happy that they threw lots of candy. I brought cold drinks plus remembered to bring a wet washcloth to sponge off Houston's face. The sun was going to be very hot and I was concerned that he would get overheated. So many of our friends stopped to talk and of course tease Houston, or should I say, Houston teased them. Boris was making his rounds and happened to spot us.

"No goot Amedican voman bothering Houston," he playfully mocked then continued on his way.

After the parade we all headed over to the festival several blocks away. There were so many food booths and mobs of people. Houston was able to maneuver his wheelchair through the crowds without running over anyone. He said later, "I managed to only hit one old lady and a dog." He even tried to show off by putting his chair in fourth gear. That was the gear he liked to use in the skywalk in the winter when I had to run to keep up. He had told me I needed to get some exercise!

🍁   🍁   🍁

The phone rang in the middle of the night. Steve sleepily answered then handed the phone to me. My agency was calling saying that Mrs. McMann had called 911 and the emergency crews that went over there couldn't understand what she wanted. They asked me to go over and see if I could figure out what was going on. I looked at the clock—2:30 AM.

"Yes," I said. "I'll be there as soon as I can get dressed." I was wide awake now, full of curiosity.

Telling Steve not to worry, that I would be home as soon as I got her settled, I got myself ready and headed out the door. I could only imagine what she was doing to these poor paramedics. It would take about 20 minutes to drive to that part of town. When I started up her street I could see red lights flashing from three police cars and an ambulance parked in her driveway. I got out of my car as the ambulance crew began coming down the sidewalk towards me.

They laughingly said, "We checked all her vitals and everything seems fine."

"I'm sure they were!" I replied with a chuckle.

They continued, "We've never met anyone like her before."

"I'm sure you haven't," I laughed while agreeing with them.

"Oh, by the way," they added, "we called her son and he's on his way."

Oh, no! This was J.T. the son she was always criticizing. She wouldn't be happy to hear that he had been called! I had never met him before so couldn't wait to see what he really was like in person. Who would have thought I would meet him in the middle of the night!

I thanked the police and medical staff as they were leaving and walked in the house. Mrs. McMann was sitting up in her bed with the table lamp on, looking as regal as ever. I asked with some concern, "Are you okay?"

"Does it look like I'm okay?" she answered in a huff. "I couldn't find my scuffs so I tried to call you. I didn't have your number so I thought of my dear friend the police chief whose number was 9-1-1 and that's when I called him. But who do I get but these crazy people running around here and they were no help at all!"

I looked around the room and saw that some of the medical equipment from the ambulance crew had been left.

"Oh dear." I said with alarm. "They've left their bag and they might need it soon."

"Not a problem," she said. "Just call 9-1-1."

"No!" I hastily exclaimed, "We won't do that again! I'll just look up their number in the book." I searched the yellow pages and came up with a non-emergency number to call. Soon they returned shamefacedly to get their equipment. I met them at the door and handed their supplies to them. I'm sure, because of their unusual encounter with this woman, they had been distracted from their routine.

Heading back in her bedroom I remembered I needed to forewarn Mrs. McMann that her "dear" son was on his way. When I told her that he had been called, she angrily retorted, "I had all these crazy people running around and he's the craziest of them all!" She was not very happy with the thought of him coming.

I asked her what were these "scuffs" that she had been searching for, knowing this was the reason she had called 9-1-1 to begin with. She acted like I was crazy for not understanding what they were. I began looking around for who knows what. I turned down the covers on her bed and asked, "Why are your slippers under your sheets?"

"Oh, there they are!" she exclaimed with relief, "Wonder who put them there!"

I guess I had found her "scuffs," the reason for all the commotion!

Just about that time I heard a car screeching down the street. I figured it must be J.T. so I went to the front door to look out. There was a white S.U.V. careening up the driveway and coming to a screeching halt and a distraught looking man in his mid 50's jumped out with his hair flying in all directions. Before he came in I tried to diffuse the situation by quickly telling him that it wasn't her idea to call him. I explained that the whole thing was a terrible mistake and I made sure he realized that the paramedics shouldn't have asked him to drive there.

He seemed bewildered while listening to my explanations but when I paused for a moment he threw his hands up in the air, then looked at me as if he were pleading and asked, "What am I to do with Mama?" Here he was, a CEO in a big corporation and he was asking me for advice? He appeared to be at his wits end.

He followed me in the house and began giving his mother a scolding. Of course his remarks didn't sit well with her so she had plenty of expletives to give him in return!

Before he left he mentioned to me he had heard she had been trying to drive again and we would have to do something to keep her from undertaking this dangerous task in the future. I agreed and said I would take her as many places in my car as I could, that is, if she would allow me. He continued talking and said he had tried to persuade her to move to a retirement home but she wouldn't hear of it.

"Over my dead body!" she retorted each time he brought the subject up.

I told him my opinion was that a person was better off if they were kept in their own home as long as possible if their welfare was not compromised. Usually one was happier in one's own surroundings, not to mention the care being cheaper. He seemed satisfied, for the present. He said we'd discuss the matter a little later and he drove off. Not much time would pass before I was to see him again.

🍁 🍁 🍁

Houston entertained me with stories from the time he served in the army between the Korean and Vietnam War. He must have been a character because he ended up in so many accidents due to his drinking. Once he drove a jeep over a cliff but was able to get out and climb back up the steep embankment unharmed. Another time he drove an army tank through the motor pool. He almost got court-marshaled for that one but instead they transferred him to a different platoon with the idea that others needed to share these mishaps! What a way to get even with a rival squadron!

He must have straightened out because he eventually became a drill instructor. I could see him barking orders at everyone! One day he was instructing his platoon on how not to get blown up in a land mine and as Murphy's Law would have it, he accidentally stepped on one and got "blown up." He was in the hospital for months and had to have reconstructive surgery, yet his family never knew about it. They never even knew he got a purple heart! I guess this honor wasn't something he wanted to brag about.

"Where is your Purple Heart?" I asked one day.

"I threw it away!" he replied wryly.

"What! Why did you do that?" I asked in surprise.

"It wasn't anything you could eat!" This was what he said whenever he meant that something wasn't "useful." I was still so amazed that after all he had been through he still had such a good attitude. However I still liked to tease him about being grumpy and needing an attitude adjustment.

"When Steve was in the Army," I told him, "he stayed in officer's barracks called BOQ's. What were the one's called that you stayed in?" I asked him.

"Foxholes!"

I was never prepared for his fast witty quips.

Soon I began to wonder why he wasn't getting any veteran benefits with all the years he had served. After many phone calls with me inquiring how to go about getting some, we were finally given an appointment for an evaluation but that would involve having to travel about 70 miles to a large veteran's facility. We were gone almost an entire day since he needed a physical plus an eye exam. We also had to meet with the special department that set up guidelines for those with disabilities like his. While waiting for each appointment we noticed so many others with similar disabilities. Our efforts paid off because a few months later [The Army doesn't do anything quickly] we were assured that they would start sending us some of his medical supplies along with most of his prescriptions. What a shame that he hadn't been able to get any help sooner than this.

The boxes of supplies started coming each month. Boris helped me carry them up to Houston's apartment since they had been delivered in the Security area.

"Amedican voman need to verk harder weeth these supplies," he teased.

I took note that if he had really wanted me to work harder, he would have had me carry the boxes up myself. I was at least glad to see that Houston was saved hundreds of dollars with these provisions.

Most of my patients had caller ID and even though I wasn't supposed to give out my home phone number, mainly for my own protection, I found out later that some had written the number down after I had called to get directions to their house. Apparently Houston's son had seen the number and had programmed it in his father's phone so that he could call me by just pressing one number.

I really didn't mind most of the time but a few times he called just as we were sitting down to dinner. He had dropped his fork and couldn't eat his dinner, or maybe he just needed to be propped up a little more in bed. Several times I felt myself starting to feel a little irritated, mostly that he hadn't called his son who was only three blocks away but didn't want to bother him. Then I began to feel guilty and immediately said I would be there right away. Sometimes I asked if he could wait until we finished eating but other times it seemed urgent enough for me to go right then.

My family was very understanding for the most part so they told me to go ahead and leave. I had a 45 minute round trip, counting the time parking, walking down the ramp to enter the building then waiting for the elevator. His appreciation was always so evident and that made me really glad I had driven down there. I know he was relieved not to have to bother his son. What a lesson to me of how often we take for granted just the simplest things such as being able to get into a more comfortable position in bed!

Sam was the older man who came in the evenings to get Houston to bed. Several times I had to substitute for him when he needed to go out of town but by then I was used to doing the reverse routine of getting him ready to retire. The pillows had to be adjusted just the right way, he needed propped up on one arm in order for him to be able to eat his supper in bed, and his pills were to be arranged on his radio.

After disassembling one side of his wheelchair to make possible his transfer into bed, I had to drive the chair back across the room and then relocate another special chair next to his bed for support. He wanted his TV turned to the right channel with the remote nearby, and a washcloth laid out to cover his eyes to keep out the glare. His special evening routine was simple yet helped him cope with the long hours until he was able to fall asleep.

🍁   🍁   🍁

At the same time Mrs. McMann was becoming more and more demanding. She had choice words to say about everyone and I guess I counted myself lucky that she hadn't turned her wrath on me—yet! Even though she had reluctantly ridden with me a few times she was determined to get her own way by driving herself places, especially when I wasn't there.

One day her son called to ask a favor. [I was never going to forget how we met late that night at her house after she had called 9-1-1.] He was afraid that she was going to have an accident in her car and thought that maybe we'd better hide her car keys. He arranged that we could be at the house at the same time and he could bring his daughter to sidetrack his mother while we searched for her keys.

He was giggling like a naughty little boy while we both emptied out several large purses in her bedroom. He knew he would certainly catch her wrath if she found out what he was doing! We found several sets but after trying them in the car, they weren't the ones. Finally giving up we decided to go out in the garage and disconnect some wires under the hood. I wasn't there the day she tried to drive somewhere but I think the neighbors are still talking about all the language they heard coming from her garage!

Her family concluded that she was going to need more help. Since I was already booked up with other patients, they found a lady who was willing to move in and be with her around the clock. I felt sorry, ahead of time, for this woman and wondered if she knew what she was getting herself into!

Mrs. McMann definitely wasn't in favor of this change and had a fit that she was losing me. I was flattered because she had never told me she appreciated anything I did for her. But at the same time I knew that this was a compromise since she was not in favor of the alternative—being put in a home.

I told her I would stop in from time to time and would call so she seemed to appreciate this gesture even though she didn't understand why I wouldn't just leave my family to move in with her!

Just before Christmas I stopped in with a small present and a plate of cookies. She was all smiles. I asked how she was doing and got an earful about how bad her family was, how the store she went to had a conspiracy against her and would hide the kind of bread she liked until she left, and how her doctor could care less whether she lived or died. When she mentioned about the bread at the store, I was reminded of the second to the last time I had taken her there. She had looked for a certain kind of bread but they were out. She had a fit as she gave the stock boy a contemptuous look and started swearing saying he didn't know what he was doing and where did he hide her bread every time she came? He was just a teenager so I felt sorry for his being her scapegoat. I looked at him apologetically as he was left speechless.

The last time we went to that same store we walked in and she spoke to several of the workers. They smiled and were trying to be kind to her so I commented, "They sure are pleasant here."

She arrogantly replied, "Yes. When you are nice to them, they are nice to you."

I guess she really thought she had been kind to them! Although she added almost under her breath, "I guess they are just used to me!" That was more like it!

So I kept up with a few visits to see her, here and there, then in January gave her a call. I was surprised that her son answered. He hardly ever came over. I asked how she was. He paused then replied in a matter of fact voice, "She died." It was the same tone he would have used to say if he had to go out and rake leaves. I was shocked, although I shouldn't have been since she was in her 90's.

I asked what happened. He said that he told her he was going to have to put her in a home because she wasn't being cooperative but the morning he came over to take her, he found that she had died of natural causes. I was reminded that she always had told him, "Over my dead body!"

While we were talking, he quickly said, "I know my mother wasn't very easy to get along with but I want to thank you for all you did for her this past year. Is there anything in the house that you would like to have?"

Visions of her grand piano flashed before my eyes but I certainly wasn't going to ask for anything in that price category! Instead I meekly requested a copy of her regal picture displayed on the mantle of her fireplace.

As good as his word, J.T. sent the picture along with the following note,

Dear Jodie,

Sorry it's taken so long to get this to you—there has been a lot of stuff to go through. I remember with admiration and appreciation your tender care of my mother.

Best Regards,

James Travis McMann

CHAPTER 5

❁

We were headed down to the first floor main lobby to get Houston's mail. Of course we needed to stop in to see Sally and Carmen in their office right beside the mailroom. They both came over to give him a big hug and find out what he had been up to that day. They had come to another birthday party I recently had for Houston. I was pleased that many neighbors and staff who worked in the building came also and stayed quite awhile. I was hoping he would see that they really cared for him.

Houston liked to flirt with Carmen, the younger of the two, and she entertained us with some of her stories from her former days when she was in the navy. I think she was trying to "top" some of his army stories and certainly did a good job.

🍁 🍁 🍁

Janet was coming to visit Houston. She was his ex-wife's sister and they all had grown up together in the northern part of the state. Houston had a special place in his heart for Janet and I could see he was looking forward to her visit very much. He had a guest bedroom that was dreary and unwelcoming so I went to work to try to make it bright and cheery.

I talked him into letting me buy some new sheets and a comforter for the bed. Earlier I had suggested that he start setting some money aside for things like this. I told Houston we should hide some of his allowance in a drawer after Bruce brought his money each week and that way Elinor wouldn't find all of it. Every once in awhile we did that very thing, saying it was "for a rainy day" and then we jokingly referred to it as "our Swiss bank account."

I didn't think Bruce would mind if he found out and thought he might even be a little amused, especially knowing his sister was getting "cheated." I noticed he was starting to warm up a little more towards his dad plus he was always respectful of me. But we did have fun thinking we had tricked Elinor out of some of the money she thought she was entitled to. Houston's eyes seemed full of mischief when he instructed me to put some money in the drawer for these occasions.

I dragged an old small table out of the closet and found a tablecloth to fit. Perfect! There also was a lamp so I pulled that out too. I brought in some nice pictures that I previously had found at a yard sale and hung them on his bare walls then I set out some fragrant candles on the open shelf in the corner. The room was looking better already especially with the new comforter on the bed.

Houston had to come in to see for himself and kept complaining that she wasn't worth all that trouble. He didn't really mean that but always liked to put up a fuss. He always spoke highly of her so I knew it was worth the fuss. She lived in Arizona in the winter and in northern Michigan in the summer. I appreciated how she encouraged him by sending cards and giving him a call now and then.

I wasn't around when Janet arrived but I got the chance to meet her the next morning when I came to get Houston ready for the day. She not only was pleasant to be with but also had a wonderful sense of humor. No wonder Houston had looked forward to her visit!

The two of them went at it with their friendly banter and were constantly reminding each other of things that had occurred in the past. Janet seemed appreciative of the groceries that I had bought so that she could at least have something to fix for breakfast. I knew that the two of them would probably go downstairs to the restaurant for lunch and she would get to meet some of Houston's friends who worked there. Her visit was definitely going to be good for him.

She got a charge out of hearing some of his escapades. I tattled on how he had this running battle with me every morning about his slippers. He had these ridiculously ugly gray slippers that he had been wearing when I first started working for him. But one day I found a really nice pair in the closet. Apparently his parents had sent them for his birthday but he hadn't taken them out of the box. They were a moccasin type, very stylish and soft and I knew these would look better on him especially when we went for our walks. So I made him wear the new ones.

But Sam, the man who worked for Houston in the evening and weekends, let him wear the ugly ones. I sometimes brought one of the boys down to visit him on Saturdays and there he would be, looking so smug as he glanced downward to make sure I noticed he was wearing his unsightly slippers!

The same thing happened with certain clothes he insisted on wearing. He had a closet full of nice, stylish ones but he had an old favorite shirt he loved to wear all the time. Sam let him wear it every day of his life. I think we both enjoyed our verbal battles each day. I, of course, won but he made it sound like I was abusing him.

Janet's favorite story was the one I told her about Houston doing his own dental work just the week before. He had a tooth that had been bothering him but he wouldn't consent to my making an appointment for him. One day, when I wasn't there, he got a pair of pliers that he found on his windowsill and out it came!

"Houston Frederick!" she exclaimed, "What in the world were you thinking? Haven't you ever heard of a dentist?"

His lips twitched, trying to suppress a smile.

"Why would I want to go there?" he growled. All he would do would be to cause me pain and take my money.

We both could see his point but didn't want to encourage him to do more harm to his mouth.

"Houston, one of these days I'm going to read you the riot act!" she teasingly told him as she took his coffee cup over to the kitchen to refill. "Can't you ever act with decorum?"

Janet was hoping to get together with Bruce and Elinor while she was in town. I knew they would want to see her since they considered her their favorite aunt. She had tried to keep in touch with them through the years.

I was glad to have met her but wished that she lived closer so that we could become better acquainted. I had no idea at the time, how she would become one of my biggest allies when that big horrible event came crashing down on me a few years later.

She promised she would be back in the spring because that was when she and her husband moved to their cottage up north. They would stop in to take Houston out to lunch on their way through and maybe we would get a chance to visit.

🍁 🍁 🍁

It was Bruce's birthday and Houston and I were meeting him for lunch. Since we had never seen the inside, I thought Houston might like to go over to the radio studio where Bruce worked. We only had about four blocks to walk and with the day being so nice we were thrilled to get out.

Bruce and his sidekick Mark were surprised to see us there but also tickled that they would be able to show us around. The staff seemed glad to finally get to meet Bruces's dad and asked him, "Did you give your son his dry sense of humor?"

I assured them that there was no doubt about that.

After our tour we enjoyed a nice lunch across the street. Bruce appeared to be having a good birthday and laughed when he opened the gift I had picked out for his dad to give him. I had found a cute book that had the backgrounds of funny sayings, thinking he could use something like this on the air.

I had a new patient and this one was on the west side of town. The neighborhood wasn't a good one and I could see that the house was really run down when I arrived.

Mrs. Selmer was a frail, melancholy lady who spent her whole day in a wheelchair. The inside of the house was worse than the outside but since I only had an hour to be with her to do personal care, there wasn't any time left to do other things.

She had a lot of medical problems that needed attention. But during this hour she asked if I would go down in the basement and start a load of wash. I didn't mind and was only happy to help her out. I made my way down the creaky old wooden steps and in the dim light could barely make out what was down there. Actually there was so much junk I wasn't even sure if I could find the washer. There were several rooms, all piled with old things, but I eventually found what I was looking for and I opened the lid to get a load started.

For some reason I started to get this feeling that I wasn't alone. The feeling passed then I felt silly, thinking it must have just been my imagination. I quickly made my way over to the stairs and went back up to try and calm my nerves while beginning work on some of my paperwork. While I was getting my papers ready for her to sign, she mentioned something about George.

I questioned, "Who is George?"

"Why, that's my good for nothing brother-in-law who lives in the basement!"

I gasped. "In the basement?" I squeaked. No wonder I had a funny feeling while I was down there!

Just then I heard footsteps coming from where I had just been. The door opened and there was a hairy, tattooed, greasy old man glaring at me. I guess I must have interrupted his "slumber" or whatever it was he was doing down there. I could only imagine what he must have been thinking as this unsuspecting health care worker had come down into his domain. I still get the creeps thinking what he could have done to me when I least suspected! I would certainly think twice before going down there again!

I had discovered, upon arrival, that Mrs. Selmer was a chain smoker. This was a serious problem because she was also on oxygen. I had a constant fight on my hands to get her to extinguish her cigarettes every time I came and sometimes hid them along with her matches.

I just knew that one day she would blow herself—and George—up, but somehow she always managed to get away with it. Ironically enough, she lived on a street by the name of Chesterfield, which was also the name of a cigarette from the 50's.

I didn't have her as a patient very long since the family decided she needed to go into a home. She definitely needed additional medical care.

A new patient in another county replaced her. He was just a few months away from being 100 and had been living all alone until he got pneumonia. I was unprepared for the primitive conditions I faced at his place. I felt like I was at the Little House on the Prairie. There was no running water. The gray lofty farmhouse was older than he was and had never been painted. I was given directions that led me many miles out in the country. I was sure I was going to get my mini-van stuck in the ruts of the dirt road each time I drove up the winding tree lined road leading to his house.

The day I arrived the wind was blowing so hard that his thin filmy curtains were horizontal most of the time I was there! I found out later that the gaps around the windows were so wide that in the summer bees buzzed in and out.

I had to pump the water then heat it if I wanted hot water. There was junk piled up everywhere and the calendars on the wall had yellowed, dating back to World War I. An old tattered farmers almanac was resting on top of some worn out magazines and that gave me a clue as to what he had done for a living. His gnarled hands and face told the story of how he had labored all of his life as a farmer. But one could tell, though, that the hard work had given him character and determination. Herman was his name. He had a dry sense of humor and his words were few but when he talked, one paid attention because what he had to say was usually worth listening to.

His daughter met me at the door that first day and she explained some of the duties I would have. She looked ancient herself so I was surprised later to find out she had just recently been married. I asked where she met her new husband and she replied, "At my mother's funeral last year. He's my cousin!" I tried not to look too surprised, but chuckled later when I thought about it. I couldn't wait to tell Houston because he was always making fun of the fact that I was from West Virginia. [I sometimes would tell about my patients but didn't mention their names to protect their identity].

Herman was so independent that it was an effort to gain his confidence. But eventually he got used to the fact that he needed some personal care from others. We got along just fine. I really looked forward to our visits one day a week and found out that he did too.

Houston's daughter Elinor was off from work again. I asked Houston if she were sick but he rolled his eyes and murmured, "In the head."

I looked at him reproachfully and said, "Now behave yourself. That's not nice to say about your daughter!"

As it turned out this continually happened time and time again, where she could get her mother to write a note saying she needed some time off due to psychiatric reasons. Since her mother was a psychotherapist with a different last name, her employer didn't know otherwise. Therefore they would give her the time off with pay. I wasn't sure what the problem was and didn't feel like it was my right to know so I left it at that. Her brother Bruce even made some unkind remarks about his sister's lack of work ethics but I just tried to let his criticisms go in one ear and out the other.

It was my birthday. Somehow Houston had arranged to get his son to buy a present to give me and there it was, all wrapped and waiting for me on the dresser in his bedroom. I was so astonished, wondering how he had remembered, but it wasn't surprising with a mind like he had. The gift consisted of an assortment from my favorite Bath and Body shop plus a gift certificate for a manicure and facial massage. How wonderful! He seemed pleased to see my excitement and gruffly said how glad he was to have me work for him. I could tell he was getting a lot of pleasure out of seeing me happy.

An hour later, after I got him up and ready for the day, I thanked him again for the nice gift then went down to the parking garage. Sitting on the hood of my mini van was another present. How strange. Who else knew it was my birthday?

I opened the van door then brought the present inside to unwrap, full of curiosity. The card surprised me when I saw it was from Bruce and his girlfriend Tonya. They thanked me for all I had done the past two years for their dad and hoped I had a good birthday. How nice! They had given me a set of candles that had coffee beans embedded in the sides. They had the aroma of hazelnut coffee and I knew they would look and smell nice in my living room at home. I smiled as I set them in the floor and turned on the engine to go to my next client's house. What a nice day this was turning out to be!

Later that day, I quickly drove back to get Houston ready for an appointment at our local Veteran's Center. When we had been to the larger one a year before they had required a reevaluation every year and said we could do that locally.

I went to his parking spot and then pulled his specially equipped van around to the front of his apartment building. I thought we could incorporate work with pleasure since the day was quite nice for April. I had packed a lunch to take with us and thought we could have a picnic as we tried out the new nature trail on the premises of the Veteran's Center.

Being early, we were glad not to be rushed for our appointment. We drove to the facility, parked, and then I lowered the ramp of his van so that we could begin our walk on the nature trail. Some volunteers had done an amazing job of transforming a wooded area into a convenient park for those who might find it difficult to walk very far.

There were birdhouses located throughout the trail and the landscaped areas were well marked, telling what kinds of bushes, trees, and flowers were planted. The trees shaded our path and soon we came to a bench. Several rays of sun peaked through the tree limbs while we ate our picnic lunch. Houston seemed extremely happy to be out in the woods. Those years spent with the D.N.R. had made him appreciate nature and it's surroundings. I silently promised myself to make more of an effort to bring him to surroundings such as this one.

His reverie was broken when I reminded him it was time to go for our appointment. We were told to begin with the Mental Health Department before we were sent to various other locations. I couldn't pass up teasing him as I said, "How appropriate that they are sending you here first!"

He gave me that look that I was beginning to know very well!

While we were waiting to be seen, an agitated man by the name of Gerald walked over to the desk.

"I want a different diagnosis!" he demanded belligerently.

The receptionist looked up with a startled expression on her face. "I beg your pardon?" she said.

"I said, I want a different diagnosis!" he repeated with a louder voice that was starting to crack with emotion.

"Why is that?" she surprisingly asked.

"Because I don't like the one they gave me!"

We were still laughing about that incident in the years to come! We finally finished with all of our appointments and he was all set for another year of veteran's benefits.

❦   ❦   ❦

The motorized wheelchair needed adjustments now and then so we made our way over to the Rehab place to have them work on it. Our good friend, Michael, always seemed to know just what was wrong. There was only one time we had to leave the chair for several days to have more parts ordered and that meant Houston had to be confined to his bed all those days. As difficult as that was, the return of the chair brought his freedom back and made him so grateful to be able to get out and about.

He complained about his "wimpy" bell that came with his chair.

"What I really need is an air horn so I can sneak up behind old ladies!" he said with a gleam in his eye.

"You wouldn't dare," I teased.

"Oh, wouldn't I?"

That gave me an idea to look for a more appropriate bell he could use. Jordan and I went out shopping one day and came across the perfect one. It was an old fashioned bell that used to go on bikes. He seemed pleased when we put it on for him and he began playing with it right away.

That afternoon I took him for a scheduled appointment at the Veteran's Outpatient Clinic. This time we didn't start out on the nature trail, but instead I wanted to show him their beautiful cemetery on the north end of the premises. I had just recently discovered this gorgeous spot on one of my bike trips with Jordon.

I parked his van in the outpatient parking lot. After lowering the ramp with his wheelchair, we headed over to the entrance. We lingered for a moment by the pond, just long enough to watch the ducks swim over to us looking for food.

Next we headed up the narrow paved path that wound itself around beautifully wooded trees. A lone squirrel scampered across the path in front of us.

We both enjoyed reading some of the names on the gravestones. He couldn't actually make them out but could see that many were so old that the elements had made them totally smooth. But there seemed to be a newer section, at least a portion where the gravestones looked brand new. We got a little closer and saw that these must have been replaced because most dated back to 1898.

"Look at this one," I eagerly said. "Her name was Jerusha. In fact, this whole section seems to be just women and most of them have such old fashioned or unusual names."

"Read off more to me," Houston said with enthusiasm.

"Well, there are two Phoebe's listed, along with a Sylvia and an Ida. It appears that most of these were during the period of the Spanish American War. Didn't you serve in that one?" I teasingly questioned.

"Watch it!" he replied trying his best not to smile.

"Oh, here's one marked Rosea Rose," I continued. "That's interesting! And next to her is Tilie and Eunice. There's also a Sophronia, Clerinda, and Clemindza."

We were thoroughly engrossed with trying to imagine what these ladies must have been like and what kind of stories they would have had to tell, that we hardly noticed the time. We barely got started in the Civil War section when I realized we had better get moving before we missed our appointment.

We left that day, feeling as if we had revisited history.

One day Houston called my home. This time it wasn't for a request to come and pick up something or readjust his pillows. He had a catch in his voice and said he had some upsetting news that he wanted to share. He had just heard that Bruce had broken up with his longtime girlfriend. I was surprised to hear the emotion in his voice but knew his relationship with Bruce and Tonya had taken a change for the better in the last few months.

At the time we didn't know any details but wanted to make sure that Tonya knew we still cared about her no matter what had happened. We ended up leaving several messages on her answering machine, then after about a week were able to get in contact with her personally to meet for coffee. She was devastated, of course, and seemed to be grateful to have us to ventilate on.

"Jodie, I just can't believe he would do this to me after all these years!" she cried.

I'm sure she was extremely hurt to know that he already had another girlfriend to replace her. Houston wasn't normally a sympathetic person but I could tell that he was touched. He was beginning to be more involved in their lives so this breakup was particularly upsetting to him. Before she left that day, I hugged her and told her that we would keep in touch. She thanked us both and told us we would never know how much our friendship meant to her. We did keep in touch and she seemed to be a little better each time we saw her. I could tell she was trying to move on and I knew that was for the best.

🍁   🍁   🍁

It was wedding day. Elinor was getting married again. Bob, her groom, was a nice looking young man and seemed pleasant enough. Houston remarked with slight revulsion, "Wonder what he sees in her!"

"Houston Frederick!" I exclaimed with a chuckle, "Why are you being so cynical?"

"I may be cynical but it's true!" he exclaimed.

"Oh Houston, you are always so full of doom and gloom!" I quipped.

He resigned himself to letting me get him all dressed up for the wedding, after resisting my suggestions of what to wear. Actually this was kind of a compromise since he absolutely refused to wear a suit. A sports jacket would have to do and of course a tie. I had never seen him dressed up before and he looked quite nice. Of course he tried to get me to put on those awful slippers but I wouldn't give in!

I mentioned, "Houston, was there ever a time when you obeyed me without putting up a fuss?"

A "humph" sound escaped his lips as he became even more eager to defy me.

"You just like being devious," he finally stated.

"Now how is dressing up being devious?"

"Humph…"

The wedding was held in the party room on first floor so that was convenient for us. Elinor's four children were all in attendance and they looked nice as they were all dressed up for the occasion. Tonya was there also. I'm sure she must have felt awkward, especially with Bruce and his new girlfriend in attendance. There may have been around twenty guests in all but there was only one that I was looking out for—Noreen, Houston's ex-wife.

I decided that there was nothing to be fearful of, even after all he had told me, so I decided I would treat her pleasantly and definitely not stir up any trouble. When I did spot her, I noticed that her hair was tied back in a rather severe manner and her eyes narrowed as she glanced around and saw us enter the room. I didn't get a chance to talk to her until after the reception.

I observed that LeAnn, Bruce's new girlfriend was there. We had seen her on a couple of occasions but found her to be cold and distant, not at all like Tonya. But I guess we weren't being fair to compare.

After the reception Houston seemed tired so I took him up and put him to bed. He reached over to grab some Tums and also some headache pills that were on his radio.

"Aren't you feeling well?" I asked.

"Between Elinor and my "ex" I need both of these," he growled.

"Well, I know your daughter was glad that you went to the wedding."

"Glad that I paid for it, you mean," he retorted.

"Take your Tums and Exedrin and I'll see you in the morning," I smiled as I covered him up and gave him a playful punch in the arm.

"And seeing 'her'," he added while referring to his ex-wife, "made my flesh crawl!"

I returned to the party room since I had told Elinor I would help her mother clean up in the kitchen.

No one else but Noreen seemed to be helping so this seemed to be a good time to get a little acquainted. I introduced myself but of course she already knew about me and made some sarcastic remark like, "Cleaning up from the wedding has got to be a much nicer chore than having to put up with that man!"

I must have looked surprised not liking the sound of her innuendo, so I stated, "No, I really enjoy being with him. He's quite a character." Later on I was hoping she didn't take that remark the wrong way, thinking I meant a "character" as not being unique but being someone no one could stand. I'm sure that it was her inclination to believe the latter. Meeting her that day certainly was disconcerting for me. But we really weren't around each other that long.

🍁   🍁   🍁

October had come and gone. Houston surprised me by saying he'd like to get a jumpstart on his Christmas shopping. I very delightedly said

I had the afternoon off the following day and if he felt up to it, I would take him to our new mall. He tried to fuss and fume but I knew deep down he really wanted to go. What a change from the year before when he had to be convinced to buy his family gifts!

The afternoon was brisk so I bundled him up and we headed out to his van. The mall was already filled with early Christmas shoppers and the stores were decorated for the season. Soft carols were being played and everyone seemed in a festive mood.

We were only able to shop in four stores, due to the crowds, but we had great success and felt an accomplishment when we were done. As we gathered up our purchases, we stopped at a stand for a cinnamon pretzel and coffee. Houston glanced up at me with a dazzled look in his eye as he remarked, "I feel like I'm in sensory overload!" I hadn't realized this was his first visit to a mall in over twenty years! No wonder he felt that way! I probably would have chosen our smaller mall if I had realized that, but what did it matter, as long as he had a good time.

CHAPTER 6

Three years had passed and I was settling into a steady routine with my patients. Arnie and Erma treated me like one of the family and I really felt like I had known them all my life. Arnie's sense of humor was contagious. We did a lot of laughing during my hours at their house. I think this must have been therapeutic for him because, sad to say, we were noticing more and more that dementia was creeping into Erma's life. Her memories were fading away into a fog.

She was the same age as Arnie, who had just turned 85 but she insisted that she was only 83 and that he was adding wrong.

"Arnie!" she exclaimed, "You need to go back to school to learn how to count!"

Her statement got us tickled and pretty soon she was laughing with us, not really knowing why.

Arnie and the family were always trying to get Erma to go for a walk, saying it would strengthen her and help her to heal. She would go only when she felt like it and that wasn't too often. One day she began putting on her shoes as if to go out. Arnie asked, "Erma, where are you going?"

"Why, I'm going out for a walk," she replied.

"But it's snowing outside and I haven't shoveled yet!" he exclaimed.

"Why not!" she retorted. "Get out there and get started!"

Reluctantly Arnie put on his coat, hat, gloves and boots to go out and begin his long tedious chore. It also involved having to clean off the back deck and handicapped ramp that the family had built to make her exit a little easier. He shoveled for nearly an hour and came in all out of breath.

"Erma, you can go out for your walk now. I've finished shoveling," he panted.

"Go out for a walk! Are you crazy??? Don't you know it snowed last night?"

Poor Arnie! It was all I could do to keep from laughing when I saw the look of exasperation on his face.

My other patients seemed to look forward to my visits, and we had a great time together. Most of them agreed that it was hard for them to have strangers come in to do the things that they used to manage for themselves. Sometimes they had to get adjusted to several different people since the agency wouldn't send the same person each time.

I was glad to have regular hours with the same patients and that gave us both a sense of stability. But I did have a few people here and there that I didn't have on a regular basis. I was glad of that since many of them wouldn't have worked out. One assignment had me on my hands and knees scrubbing the floor, then trying to scrounge up food to feed this very hungry little boy while his mother was "entertaining" men in her bedroom. I was also suspicious that she was dealing in drugs so after reporting the situation to my agency, they didn't send anyone else back to help. The Welfare Department had opened the case and I guess they weren't aware of what was going on.

One lady expected me to clean out her dog kennels. I know my agency would have frowned on her request because heavy cleaning wasn't in my job description but I did it anyway just to please her. She had long-haired collies that she let run loose in the house. Every time I went over, which was only once a week, her carpet was filled with dog hair and the vacuum bag had to be changed frequently because of clogging.

The second time I tried to change it, she lost her temper and accused me of manually stuffing dog hairs into the vacuum bag, as if I had little else to do. Needless to say, that was the last time I was there. I decided I wasn't going back.

Another job landed me in the facilities of a mental health ward with my duties being to teach personal hygiene to some of the patients. I thought I had a lot of patience but later on decided that I was in dire need of lots more. One patient bit and kicked me as he rolled around on the floor. I went away with bruises and marks all over my legs and arms.

A different job was helping a mentally challenged man who had a criminal record. He had been injured at work and needed physical therapy along with transportation and some social service work. One day I had to take him to the Secretary of State office to get an identification card. When they typed in his name, sirens and red lights started to go off. I pretended not to be with him but later asked why this had happened. He sheepishly admitted he had a "few" extra infractions against him such as crashing up several police cars!" Not too long after that he was back in prison for violation of parole.

I'll never forget the "Rat Man." He had been in the hospital with a torn up arm from a work related incident. Actually, I think a garbage truck hit him while he was on the job. Workman's Comp contacted my agency and they opened the case while he was still in the hospital. That explained how I could be sent to such a horrible dwelling. I was sure I had the wrong house when I pulled up because there must have been forty garbage bags piled on the front porch. I double-checked the house number and to my dismay saw it was the right one.

A stocky man in his late 40's came to let me in. His arm was all bandaged up from his recent surgery but that wasn't the first thing I noticed. My eyes wandered past him to a site to behold. More garbage bags—only these filled the living room. There was a six inch wide path that allowed a person to pass through but only if one went sideways! The bags were stacked on top of each other up to my eye level. The stench from the room was almost more than I could bear. Later I found out he had been living there with his invalid mother and she had been incontinent. Apparently nothing had been cleaned after she passed away.

I had several duties. Not only was I to change the dressings on his arm but I was to fix some lunch for him, do errands, and maybe some laundry. I reluctantly inched my way into the kitchen. My shoes made crunching noises as I was stepping on heaven knows what. I wondered why there was brown rice all over the counters so right off the bat grabbed some wet paper towels and tried to clear off a space so I could fix him something to eat. It wasn't until the next day that I discovered what this brown rice was!

I had to go downstairs to put in a load of laundry. The basement was more like a cellar with lots of cobwebs and a very dismal light. Something darted past me and I jumped. I was hoping it wasn't what I thought it was, but I was wrong. Here came another one—a huge rat!

I immediately ran upstairs and put a call through to my boss because at that point I was concerned for my health. I was sure she would immediately pull me from the case. Not so! Actually I got very little support.

She reminded me, "Jodie, don't you have your Haz Mat kit?"

I had forgotten that when I started work three years earlier they had given me a clear plastic pouch with a mask, goggles, gloves, along with head and foot coverings to use in tough situations. I had been sure that this one crossed the line especially when I had already been exposed to who knows what the day before.

The "Rat Man" had gone upstairs so I was able to talk a little more freely with trying to describe how bad the house was. Still she didn't budge and kept repeating, "I won't be able to get anyone else to do the job so you'd better stick it out."

That showed me she was more interested in keeping this job with the agency rather than having concern for her employee!

When I left that day I wondered how I could ever be able to go back, yet I knew I had to since she had ordered me to return and "clean up the mess." I was sure she had thought I was exaggerating. This man was oblivious as to what others might have thought about his house and I really think that having lived like that for so long, he didn't see any problem.

I went back for three whole days and wore my Haz Mat outfit. After the third day I couldn't even see that I had made a dent with all that needed to be done. But I did find out that someone from his church had brought him a meal and having seen the condition of the house, reported back to others in the parish. They in turn contacted a professional company.

Three different agencies took one look and turned down the job! The fourth one came in and not only accepted the challenge but also did a fabulous job totally filling up two large dumpsters. One of the women, and there were several working, said this was the worst house she had ever encountered! Of course by the time everything was cleaned up, my duration working for this man had ended. My agency was probably at the moment trying to decide which nightmare case to give Jodie. I certainly wouldn't be that eager to see what would be in store for me!

🍁 🍁 🍁

My car needed replaced. Since I had been travelling all over the county and going into some hard to get places I needed something with four wheel drive. Steve and I went shopping one weekend and found a good used S.U.V. It just suited my needs and I was thrilled to finally get something dependable. I was remembering the year before when I had gotten stuck about 45 miles out in the country. Thank goodness for my sack of kitty litter that I sprinkled under my tires for traction. I would have been there until Spring.

Houston wanted to hear every detail of what my new truck looked like and how it drove. I told him that when the weather got warmer we would go out in the parking garage and he could get a good look but he wasn't allowed to race me.

He seemed extra happy one day. Janet had just written and told him she was on her way from Arizona and would stop by for a visit. I was elated too since we hadn't seen her in awhile. I quickly went about getting her room ready and hoped I'd be around when she came. I did miss her arrival but got back in time to join them for coffee downstairs in the café.

We hugged and tried to get caught up on all that had transpired since we last had seen each other. Houston mumbled something about not being able to get a word in edgewise but I think he was more concerned that I would tattle on all the things he had been up to, which of course I did. Janet laughed again at his latest antics. I very delightedly told how he had taken a different woman out to eat every day the week before, how he had been sneaking and eating junk food that had spoiled his appetite, and (the most recent) that he had been getting late night phone calls from an old girlfriend who had buried four husbands. Janet pretended to fuss at him but then knew it was all in vain after seeing his mischievous but defiant look.

"Houston Frederick! I guess you will never change!"

It would soon be four years since I had started working with Houston. His Multiple Sclorosis flared up now and then to cause complications but for the most part he had remained healthy these years that he had been in my care.

He reminded me of some of his long hospital stays in the past and how many months he had to endure being in a hospital bed. When these flare-ups occurred, normally his skin areas were the first to be affected and start to break down. His sores were a constant battle because he couldn't change his position in bed and I couldn't be there often enough to turn him. I knew that we had been fortunate, in the four years knowing him, that he hadn't been admitted to the hospital.

That's how we found ourselves having to make a little more visits than usual to the wound care clinic. The staff members in this office considered Houston to be one of their favorite patients so it was nice to see them make over him and pretend to scold him when he made some mischievous remark. The doctor came in and made the usual statement as to what good care I was giving him. Houston always had some funny quip to say in return. Then the doctor instructed me with what kind of new treatment we would try this time. Again he reminded me that with M.S. cases the treatments would work for a period of time then stop and they would have to try something different.

※　　※　　※

Todd, my oldest son, had just joined the Air Force Reserves and they were going to pay his way through college. He had started college but after the first semester had to take a break in January to go to Basic

Training in San Antonio. I was sure that his time there would be very difficult for him especially since he didn't like being away from home.

We didn't hear from him for the longest time but we eagerly read his first letter when it arrived and had to chuckle at some of his comments:

Dear Mom and Dad,

I am doing fine but I don't really like it down here. Everybody is very mean. We are not allowed to talk or take any free time. [Apparently he was sneaking this letter off to us!] They give us exactly three minutes to eat each meal. [What was he complaining about? That's how fast he always ate at home!] I am always hungry because I never have enough time. They put out all these wonderful desserts, knowing we won't have time to eat them so our mouths are always drooling. Actually we have to almost unhinge our jaws like my snake and swallow the food whole!

I never know what my schedule is because they won't tell us. Last week, which they called zero week, we did a lot of marching and had classes. I sure didn't expect the T.I.'s [Technical Instructors] to be this mean! They come in during the middle of the night and wake us up for no reason. Also the planes from the Air Force base down the street always fly over us and they are very loud.

Dad, you made it sound like we got some time to ourselves every once in awhile but we don't. We can't even write letters when we are waiting in line.

The days have been going by very slow. The best part of the day is the five-mile run ending with a couple hundred pushups. I am looking forward to Warrior Week which will be coming up soon. That is when we camp out in tents and pretend to be at war. We will get to shoot the M16's and use the gas chambers.

Oh, I forgot to mention that when I arrived here in San Antonio, it was 11:30AM and I had to wait until 7:30PM to get picked up. How boring!

I miss everyone so much.

Love, Todd

I took this letter with me the following day to read to some of my patients. Houston, especially, got a charge out of it, remembering his time in the Army when he was a Drill Instructor himself.

He commented, "Do you plan on going down for his graduation from Boot Camp?"

I told him that, yes, we had decided we were going to take the train and turn it into a family vacation, which we hadn't had in a long time.

"Sounds like a lot of fun," he remarked longingly.

Several more letters came. My favorite was the third one. He wrote:

Dear Mom and Dad,

I am still very homesick. Every day is so tough here. They are always telling us that if we mess up we will get recycled, meaning you have to start all over with Basic Training! I know of some guys that actually had to do that for such a minor thing!

Our Squadron's name is Alcatraz because it is so tough. There are 8 other Squadron's but one of them is nicknamed Candyland since they get dessert and 15 minutes to eat! I was able to eat there today because I had an appointment in personnel.

I ate 5 pieces of fish, 2 hot dogs, 1 hamburger, a piece of pie, an ice cream sandwich, a bowl of ice cream and a cinnamon roll. It tasted so good and almost made up for the past 3 weeks when I didn't have time to eat. [I was glad Uncle Sam was paying for this meal!]

CHAPTER 7

Breathing seemed to be a little difficult for Houston one day. Since his cough had worsened in the night, I told him to make sure he let the nurse, who was coming in the next hour, know how bad he felt.

The nurse came and seemed concerned about Houston's condition so she put a call through to Bruce suggesting that he take his dad to get a chest x-ray. I got a call from Bruce a little while later informing me that he was on his way to the hospital with his Dad and they were just going to get him checked out. He wondered if I could come and meet them as soon as I finished my last job. I assured him I would be there as soon as I could.

I was full of apprehension as I drove to the hospital and tried to tell myself not to be too alarmed, reminding myself that he had experienced a good four years of not having to be admitted, but I still didn't want anything to happen to him. He had told me of so many horrible experiences and I knew he would be fearful that they would be repeated now.

I found myself reflecting over the past four years and my mind was occupied with so many thoughts. I had refused to accept the fact that his days might be numbered even though he had already lived long past the projected time frame of most Multiple Sclorosis sufferers. What would it be like without him? I didn't even want to know! He had given me a new meaning on life. He somehow had the ability to bestow on many people a different perspective. How could one grumble about some petty thing such as some inconvenience they encountered while standing in line at the grocery store? How could one complain of tossing and turning in bed at night due to not being able to sleep, when he was never even able to change his position until someone came in the morning to move him? The list was endless as to the new relevance in life he had given me!

So it was with these thoughts in mind that I parked my truck in the parking lot at the hospital and hurried in to find the x-ray department. Bruce met me out in the hallway and directed me back into the tiny room where they were awaiting the results.

In the meantime one of the nurses had taken his vital signs and seemed to think the problem wasn't as bad as we had initially thought. We were relieved but still wanted to be on the safe side.

A doctor came in and reconfirmed what the nurse had observed. He suggested that we just keep an extra eye on him but be sure and bring him back if he had any more spells. Houston almost had a smile on his face after that remark! He wasn't about to remain there if he had any say in the matter!

Bruce seemed relieved that I had come because I was the only one that knew how to assemble and disassemble his wheelchair and that had to be done each time he was lifted in and out of it. So I got the wheelchair ready and he was lifted back in it. Bruce seemed to be in a hurry to return to work and asked if I would follow them back to the apartment and be available to put his dad to bed since Sam had been called earlier to cancel his evening visit. I told him I could and he breathed a sigh of relief.

The roads were slushy as we meandered through town, working our way back to the main street to get home. I was sure that Houston would be more than docile regarding his evening routine and probably wouldn't even put up a fuss, being so glad to be back in his apartment.

We pulled into the parking garage and I saw with dismay that Bruce's truck was parked in my space. He had parked there before driving his dad's van to the hospital. Oh well, maybe I could just pull into the empty spot next to it since I was in a rush to get Houston situated and back in bed. Besides, the people who parked in the space were hardly ever there and I would only be occupying it no longer than 20 minutes.

Bruce parked Houston's handicapped van and lowered the ramp after the wheelchair was in place. We said goodbye to his son and quickly moved indoors to go up on the elevator. I was right in that he was more manageable without any artificial gripes. I couldn't resist making the comment that it was about time he obeyed me.

He let me get him in bed without too much fuss. After I propped him up I arranged the tray with his warmed up supper I had brought earlier in the day. I reminded him of his need to eat in order to get some of his strength back. His look of meekness was foreign to me and I told myself that maybe he would be back to his old self in the morning. Certainly the hospital staff wouldn't have released him if there had been cause for alarm.

After telling him goodbye I headed back out to the parking garage, but to my dismay found a huge red violation sticker pasted on the windshield of the driver's side of my truck! Yes, I had parked in the wrong spot but ordinarily there wasn't anyone who parked there. The guys in security all knew me and were familiar with my car, but wait, I had just bought this new truck and they didn't know whom it belonged to!

I attempted to get the sticker off but the adhesive was strong and I knew I'd have to get something to scrape it. I headed down to the lower level to try to find one of the security guys to help me. I was going to tease them for putting this on my truck. They thought the whole thing was a riot when they found out I was the one they had given the violation to!

"Ha, ha, very funny," I said to them as I walked in. I gave them my lame excuse of having to park in that spot because Houston's son was in mine. Of course they had heard so many excuses through the years so weren't impressed with this one. But I knew they would be gracious with me. They knew of all the help I had been for their tenant since he was one of their favorite residents. I'm glad I gave them their laugh for the day but time was getting away from me and I needed to get home to fix supper. I was late already and knew my family would be hungry. I told them I couldn't get the sticker off, so one of the security guards said he'd give me a razor blade to use.

Back out to the parking garage I went. I knew I would have to be really careful using something that sharp. My endeavors to remove it were almost in vain as each scraping motion barely removed any of this ugly red sticker. Then there was one quick scrape and there the razor blade went, into the crevice between the windshield and the hood! Oh no! The security boys surely would be laughing at me now! Don was the ringleader in that category!

Back down I went. I sheepishly told them what happened then braced myself for their laughter, which of course they indulged themselves with. They gave me another razor blade to use again. I went back out and again the effort seemed futile. There was no quick way to get this off yet I knew I couldn't see to drive if I drove home with the sticker right in my face! I impatiently scraped just a little too hard and the blade flipped back to catch the base of my thumb! Blood spurted out and started to run down my arm. Uh oh! Now Security would be convinced I was really inept!

I quickly went around to the other side of my truck to open the side door where I usually kept paper towels. Of course they weren't there! I had carried a whole roll around for four years when I had my car, but somehow they hadn't been transferred in my truck. I had a tissue in my purse and that would have to do temporarily. I wasn't too eager to return to the Security area but knew I needed a bandaid plus someone to help me.

I am sure I gave them a whole day's worth of entertainment. I let them get their laughs then told them they needed to come out and help an old lady in distress.

I guess they must have felt sorry for me by then, because one of the guards got out the first aid kit and bandaged up my cut for me. Another one grabbed a container of Windex and a bigger blade then told me to follow him. He had a trainee with him and I knew this new person was convinced I was some kind of wacko. They joked around the whole time they were scraping and it seemed like no time at all when all the remnants of the sticker came off. I told them it served them right to be the ones to remove it since they were the ones who put it on! They thought the whole thing was a joke.

I knew I would have a good story to tell my family when I got home and would also enjoy telling Houston what had happened to me. I certainly learned my lesson and would never park where I didn't belong!

Oh how I got teased over the next few days! Houston enjoyed hearing my "parking" story as I told various embellished versions within hearing distance of several friends. One exaggerated story had them almost amputating my thumb. I had no clue how this incident was a foreshadow of things to come.

CHAPTER 8

❈

Was it *deja vu*? A week later I was working at the same lady's house at the exact time of day when I got a call from Houston's nurse saying she had called his son to come and get him and take him back to the emergency room. He was exhibiting the identical breathing and congestion problems he had the week before. I told her I would be there as soon as I could.

Before I left him that morning, he was breathing fine but his cough had worsened. I remembered seeing the opened package of an over-the-counter decongestant on the top of his TV along with some being placed by his radio with his other pills. I hadn't thought to ask where they came from but just assumed that maybe Elinor's husband had picked them up for him when he stopped by the evening before. Little did I realize how important this small detail was!

When I arrived at the hospital I found out his room number from the clerk at the information desk. I proceeded in that direction but found that Elinor had also arrived. That was a surprise. I was hoping Houston wouldn't be too irritated that she had come, although in those brief moments I could already see that she was trying to get the nurses to help her warm up her lunch that she had brought.

Bruce didn't have much patience with his sister. Most of the time he had zingers to throw out about her and certainly would have scoffed at the way she was able to have the nursing staff meet her demands. But on this occasion he was too preoccupied to pay much attention.

She continued to plead with one of the nurses saying she was following a strict diet that made her have to eat more meals during the day. If she didn't get this one in, her whole diet would be thrown off kilter. Finally one of the nurses took her bowl of soup, or whatever it was she had, and just to keep peace, went down into the nurse's lounge to warm it up in their microwave.

I, too, was only half listening but at the same time wondered if Houston was annoyed. I certainly didn't want to ask him but patted his hand to reassure him that the staff would do everything they could to help him feel better.

The doctor finally came in to examine him. He was concerned that maybe pneumonia was setting in and even though it might be the early stages, he thought it might be better to keep him overnight.

A panicked expression flickered momentarily across my client's face. I reached out to pat his hand again as I said, "This will be for the best because you wouldn't want to make another trip back to the hospital especially if you started to get worse at night. He nodded his head and had to agree with me. If he had felt better I would have teased him saying this moment had to be a "first" to have him think I was right!

Bruce turned to me and asked me a question about my daughter Holly. He had met her a few times and thought she seemed like a little "fireball." She was our oldest child that had been out of our home for five years. I chatted with him for a few minutes about some of the antics she had been up to and he chuckled saying she seemed to be a lot of fun to be around. I agreed.

Elinor finally got her bowl of soup warmed up so that kept her quiet for a little while as she guzzled it down. I was beginning to wonder why she had even come but then came up with a selfish reason. Maybe she just wanted to get away from work for awhile. She finished her lunch then bluntly stated, "I need to go out in the lobby and make some phone calls. Be right back!"

"Don't hurry," Bruce mumbled under his breath.

Bruce and I put our heads together to try to figure out the next plan. He decided to give me the keys to his dad's van in case he would be released the following day, [or whenever it would be that he was released]. That way I could just drive the van there to pick him up. He also gave me the keys to his dad's apartment and asked if I could stop in to bring some of his clothes for him to wear on the way home.

I told him I would go that very day on the way home in order to have them with me when I came the next day. I turned to Houston, smiled, and told him I would be praying that he would feel better. I also reminded him that I would be back to see him the following morning before I went to see my other patients. That way I could be with him during my regular time slot. I tried my best to rid him of any apprehension he might have of being there. He thanked me and said he would look forward to my arrival. I told him to be good and not give the nurses a hard time, which I knew he would, then I turned to leave.

I drove back to his apartment and ran into some of his neighbors as I was going to his apartment. They expressed their concern over him since they had seen the ambulance arrive earlier in the day. I told them that maybe he'd be home the following day, but in the meantime they were keeping him in for observation.

I unlocked his apartment, got the clothes, then almost as an afterthought, stopped at his Roladex to look up his parents phone number. I decided to give them a call from his apartment. They were concerned but certainly glad that I notified them. They begged me to keep them informed and I told them I would.

The next morning I went back to the hospital as I had promised and I took his change of clothes. Two nurses were in the room enjoying every minute of his teasing them. They could see the twinkle in his eyes. I was glad to see him trying to be his old self and that gave me hope that maybe he would be able to go back home that day.

But, no. The doctors wanted to keep him in because his breathing was still a little labored and his congestion was no better. They were still inclined to believe that maybe pneumonia was setting in and they didn't want to take any chances. At the same time they were puzzled that he wasn't responding to their treatment.

Each day that I went back to visit I noticed that he was getting a little worse. The vigor that he had always exhibited in the past was all gone. His eyes no longer sparkled with mischief and his energy level was practically nonexistent. Now I was really filled with apprehension.

CHAPTER 9

❀

It was Sunday, six days since Houston had been admitted. I had faithfully gone to see him every morning and evening but this day I was thinking, "My family needs me. I'll go to church with them, come home and make a nice dinner, then I will have enough time to go see him later."

With that in mind I spent some quality time with Steve and the boys, then left later on in the afternoon for the hospital. I certainly wasn't prepared for what I was about to experience that day!

I hastily made my way down the long hallway to his room. By now I was beginning to be familiar with all the surroundings. Upon entering, I immediately knew that something terrible was wrong. First of all there was no one in the room, his bed was made, and the room had been cleaned out! I paused for what seemed like a few minutes but maybe was only a few seconds, when reality came over me. I refused to believe the horror of my suspicion.

"Could it mean…that he's gone? No! I wasn't going to jump to conclusions just yet!" I thought with a catch in my throat.

I frantically sought out one of the nurses and with hesitation asked the feared question, "Can you…tell me where Houston is?"

The nurse, pausing from doing her paperwork, peered over her glasses.

"Are you family?" she quietly asked.

"Well, not really," I cautiously answered, "but I've been taking care of him for four years."

Standing up she came around to the front of the counter after seeing my panicked stricken face. "Houston took a turn for the worse this morning so he was rushed down into surgery. He stopped breathing so the family decided to put him on a ventilator."

I don't know what came over me because I'm not one to be emotional but I burst into tears and exclaimed, "I can't figure out why they didn't call and tell me!"

"Well, maybe they didn't think of it," she quickly suggested as she led me down the hall where she said the family was waiting.

I didn't know if I was crying because I was relieved that he hadn't passed away or crying because he was in such bad shape, or maybe both. Angry thoughts were running through my head, "Why wouldn't someone from the family have thought to call me? They knew I was coming back this afternoon and knew I would think the worst when I found his room like that!" I reproached myself for not coming in that morning like I usually did.

And to think that he was on life support! I knew that he had never wanted to be kept alive in such a manner and had stated that many times. I had thought he had his wishes in writing but maybe no one knew where to find the document.

I was dazed but continued to follow this nurse down the hall and was grateful that she had taken time to show me where to go. We rounded the bend and came to the surgery waiting room. Still being distraught I found myself quietly sobbing but trying to get control of my emotions as I entered the room and saw Bruce and his girlfriend LeAnn. Sitting across from them were Elinor and her husband Bob, along with their three children. To my chagrin I noticed that the room seemed to have an overpowering presence, a presence that made undercurrents ripple through the entire room. There was Noreen, Houston's ex-wife!

When Bruce saw me, as I was starting to gain my composure, he immediately got up from the corner where he had been sitting. Seeing that I was quite upset he approached me and put his arm around my shoulder. His gesture made me sob even more as I tried to tell him what I had thought when I walked into his dad's empty room a few moments earlier.

Trying to excuse what happened, he remarked, "We decided not to call you until we knew how the outcome would be."

Outcome! Hadn't we been waiting to know the outcome this past horrible week? It was a lame excuse but I forgave him and let it pass.

Up until this time Bruce had always shown respect to me. But with his mother in the room he obviously was a changed person and seemed to take on her characteristics. He began talking to me, at this point, like I was a child.

"Jodie, when my dad comes out of surgery we are going to go in one at a time to see him. But we can't let anyone in there who isn't in control of their emotions. We must maintain a positive outlook at all times so as not to upset him."

Control of my emotions!!! He had a lot of nerve! I had visited enough people in the hospital in my lifetime to know how to respond or react. I tried my best not to look at him scornfully for his quick judgment of the situation. He still failed to see how his omission of calling me with an update had unnerved me. I guess he wanted to make it sound like I was the one with the problem.

As I sank down in a nearby chair I got control of myself and looked around. The room had a surreal atmosphere. That's when I noticed that Noreen was totally taking charge of the situation. Bruce and Elinor seemed to cower under her and I looked in amazement as they did exactly what she told them to do.

"Now everyone here is going to draw him a picture so that when he gets out of surgery he will have these to look at on his wall," she barked.

Then she proceeded to tell each one of her kids and grandkids what kind of picture to draw. LeAnn was to draw a bunny, Elinor a lion, Bruce a cat...

A cat??? Didn't she know that Houston not only didn't like cats, he hated them! I, being a cat lover had found that out soon after meeting him when I told some of the naughty things my cats had done. He usually responded by telling me horror stories of what he used to do to cats when he was younger. And pictures? It might have sounded like a nice idea but all he would have been able to see was a blur. Didn't she remember he was legally blind?

Any other time I would have thought it was funny to see Bruce coloring with crayons. I still was trying to recover from the shock that I had received upstairs and therefore didn't really pay much attention except for the fact that I was the only one not making a silly drawing. Houston would have scoffed at the whole scenario!

Time clicked away. I continued sitting there, praying for that uncouth but lovable man who now was facing life and death—the moment I had dreaded for four years.

The three young grandchildren were making Elinor more irritable. The pictures were done and now they brought out snacks to eat. Well, I guess they had enough time to pack snacks but not enough time to call Jodie to at least warn her.

Apparently someone had called up north to inform the rest of Houston's family because it wasn't long before Joan, Houston's sister, breathlessly walked into the waiting room. Jumping up I grabbed and hugged her, welcoming someone who wouldn't be so hostile. Worry was written all over her face. She had come alone, not knowing how long she would need to be in town and knowing that her elderly parents wouldn't have been able to stay there for a long period of time. My crestfallen face told it all.

I briefly gave her an update on his condition and told her we were going to take turns going in to see him when he came out of surgery. I didn't mention how it was being decided in which order to go. Noreen had already been telling everyone that she was to be the one to visit him first. Oh great! That would really make him not want to pull through!

She proceeded to tell the others who would go and in what order. Of course, I was totally left out and it wasn't even mentioned that I could be the one to go last. It was a given. I didn't care. As long as I was going to get to see him I would be very patient waiting.

Joan didn't talk much, as we sat together for the long wait. She said she would assess the situation then if need be she would drive up north to pick up her parents to bring them down.

Finally, the time came for the family to take turns going in. Elatedly, Noreen stood up to be his first visitor and to mark the beginning of a quest unknown to me. We watched as she swiftly left the room feeling very important. Joan and I sat in silence, waiting for each person's turn to end.

Noreen, of course, got the most time with him, but after Bruce, Elinor and the kids went in, I nudged Joan to let her know she could feel free to go in. I knew by then he would be worn out and decided ahead of time that I would be happy with what little time would be left for me. I certainly wouldn't stay too long and definitely would keep my emotions in check!

He had been put in ICU so when I entered the room there were all kinds of monitors and equipment in operation. Indeed, his condition was grave. Remembering my reassurance to Bruce about not showing my emotions, I bravely put on a big cheerful smile and tried to be as upbeat as I could as I peered down into his sunken eyes. Sounds from the ventilator almost drowned out my words as I gently said,

"What's the meaning of this? You told me you liked nurses so now you have several at your beck and call."

He bravely looked up at me and tried to smile, unable to talk with that gruesome ventilator forcing his lungs to get oxygen.

I continued, "Would you like for me to contact Pastor Ray to come and visit you?"

He nodded strongly. So I assured him I would call as soon as I got home and arrange for him to come in. He had always told Houston to count him in as his pastor and Houston said he would be honored to.

I hesitantly asked, "Does it bother you that Noreen is here?"

He gave a contemptuous look and immediately nodded.

I suggested, "Then if it bothers you, why don't you just close your eyes when she is in the room and pretend that she's not here."

His eyes rolled and he scowled at that last comment. I knew it was easier said than done!

Noticing some wood chips by his head on the pillow, I teasingly exclaimed, "Hey, has a woodpecker been whittling away at your head?"

Bruce had walked in and hearing me say that, grunted by saying,

"No, Elinor, being of Native American descent, decided to work some of her voodoo and she also put an eagle feather above him for good luck."

Houston followed my puzzled glance upwards to see this feather, then he rolled his eyes to show that he wasn't buying into all of this ritual. That explained the incense smell permeating the room.

Having Bruce nearby reminded me that my time was up, even though I couldn't have been in there more than two minutes. I squeezed my friend's hand, told him I was praying for him and that I would be back again the following day.

Bruce followed me out in the hall. He stated that the family decided they didn't want him alone during the night so they would be making a schedule for different ones to take turns being with him. I told him to feel free to include me if he needed some coverage. He said he would.

They must have worked on some kind of schedule between the three of them, because halfway home my cell phone rang and Bruce asked me if I could take the midnight to three AM shift. I didn't hesitate to say yes even though I knew I would still have to get up to go to work the following day. I was to relieve Noreen since she was to be there until midnight.

Arriving home I quickly came in the house to find Steve. I filled him in with what had transpired that afternoon in the hospital. Retelling my experience made me relive the horror of finding his room emptied out so it was no wonder I started sobbing again almost uncontrollably. But there was no Bruce to tell me to keep my emotions in check, only Steve's comforting words along with his arms about me. Jordan was standing nearby with a look of concern on his face. I don't think he had ever seen me so upset. I knew that my whole family would be affected with whatever outcome that would occur. They also had grown close to this wonderful man.

I informed Steve that I was to go back later that evening to give the family a break from their bedside vigil. I asked Steve to locate a book of Promises that had been very meaningful to some of my clients as they were facing their last days. He found this little book for me just as I was to leave to start my shift. He assured me he would be praying not only for Houston but that I would be a comfort to him. Steve had always been impressed with the caliber of this man and I could see that he was moved.

I was reluctant to have to cross paths with Noreen but it was inevitable that I would need to see her since I was replacing her shift.

The lights were dim in ICU as I walked in but the monitors were all lit up on the various machines and equipment in the room. Noreen, acting as if I were incompetent, showed me how to sponge off his forehead and swab out his mouth, as if I hadn't been doing that for four years. I meekly let her demonstrate her former nursing abilities and tried to reassure her that I would do my best to make him as comfortable as possible.

As she gathered up her belongings I thought to mention that she might want to go a different way to the parking garage. I had noticed that the hospital's night procedure closed one area for security and made one have to walk further.

She looked at me with scorn as she coldly informed me, "I have my own parking space since I'm a Psychotherapist at this hospital."

Way to go, Jodie. Foot in mouth disease strikes again! Here I was, trying to be thoughtful in saving her some steps.

We were alone as I began to reminisce and tell him what he meant to so many people. He was in and out of consciousness but I tried to watch for signs when he was alert enough to listen. I patted his hand, adjusted his pillow, stroked his forehead, smoothed the sheets, then asked if he would like for me to read some Scripture passages that would help ease his mind. He nodded so I opened up my Promises book and turned to some pages that would give him comfort and assurance as he faced whatever fears he had.

One verse in particular caught the attention of both of us, 'Thou wilt keep him in perfect peace whose mind is stayed on thee because he trusteth in thee." (Isaiah 26:3) In the days to follow we would both need to draw on that kind of peace!

CHAPTER 10

❖

Looking back, I am so thankful we had that time together. I was oblivious to the drama that I was about to get caught up in.

The next three hours went by quickly. It was time to go so I began gathering up my book, coat and purse after LeAnn, Bruce's new girlfriend, came to relieve me of my duty. I looked at Houston's sallow face while telling him I had called his pastor friend who informed me he would be there in the morning at 8:00. I would be there also. I said goodnight and left to try to catch a few hours sleep.

I met Pastor Ray in the lobby of the hospital the following morning and we went up together to ICU. He could tell that the situation was very grim as we walked in the room. Taking Houston's frail hand he kindly mentioned how concerned everyone in his apartment building was. They had wanted him to convey a message to hurry up and get better so he could return to entertain them with his antics.

Houston put on a brave face and even tried to smile at that last comment. Our good friend asked to pray with him before it was time to leave. He asked God to continue to watch over him and to keep him from being afraid in the days to come. He also prayed in earnest that the doctors would have wisdom in how to give him the best of care so that he could soon go home.

I knew this prayer meant a lot to Houston because he looked up at Pastor Ray with the utmost respect after he had finished and I could also see that a new calmness had crept into his eyes with the reminder that he wouldn't be alone.

I told Houston I needed to leave to go to my next appointment but would return mid-day to see how he was doing. Pastor Ray followed me out in the hallway and asked me to keep him informed with his condition. He said he would be more than glad to come back, even if it meant being called in the middle of the night.

I was grateful that he could give us this kind of consolation and thanked him from the bottom of my heart.

Oh, how naïve I was. How would I have ever known what was in store for me that very day and the days to come! Sometimes it's better not to know what lies ahead. One could try to equip oneself for these situations! Later, I would remember that day and would become aware how one event changed the course of my life forever.

※　　※　　※

Arnie and Erma were patiently waiting for me when I arrived at their house. I had called to let them know I would be a little late, having stopped in the hospital first. I was glad to be with them for the morning and tried my best to get my mind to stop worrying about Houston.

I hurried back to the hospital after getting some work done for Arnie and Erma. They had seemed to sense my heavy heart and were appreciative that I still was able to help them out.

I rode the elevator up to the second floor and made my way down the corridor to Intensive Care. When I came unsuspectingly to his room, Bruce and Noreen were standing outside of his door, almost as if they were guarding it. I greeted them then said with a smile, "I was noticing that the nursing staff used Duoderm for his wound care. I know I'm not in charge of that area anymore while he is in here but you may want to double check with the Wound Care Clinic. We have found that this type of treatment is counterproductive for him."

If I hadn't been so preoccupied maybe I would have noticed Noreen bristle at my suggestion. It seemed as if she had tentacles and they were trying to extend in every direction to her benefit. But I continued on and said, "Oh, and before I forget it, Houston wanted me to contact his pastor friend to come and pray with him, which he was able to do this morning."

Noreen, looking at me with distaste, coolly stated, "Jodie, wait down in the lounge. He can't be seen right now."

Fine. I could wait if that's what she wanted. I would wait all afternoon. But sitting in the lounge with Elinor chattering away was starting to get on my nerves after the first twenty minutes. I vaguely listened as she talked incessantly, almost without taking a break to breathe, totally immersed in her own affairs. No wonder her dad would lay his phone on the pillow and let her jabber away, without even knowing there was no one listening! I used to fuss at him for doing this very thing and now I was wishing I could!

This was a private lounge that somehow Noreen had managed to arrange for her family since she was employed at this hospital. I also had heard her demand that she be given two adjoining rooms next to Intensive Care for her family to stay in, and her wish was granted. My patient was right about her power. How could I have doubted him?

Maybe a half hour passed. The door opened and in walked Bruce. I stood to my feet, anxiously awaiting any kind of update on his dad's condition but he seemed rather subdued and I noticed he avoided looking at me. Elinor and her husband gathered around him as he quietly spoke, "It has been decided that Houston [he always referred to his dad by his name rather than call him Dad] needs more privacy so, now only family members can go in to see him."

I was waiting for him to continue on by saying, "But we consider you family, Jodie, so you can go in to see him, too." That didn't happen. Silence. Next, Bob looked at me and tritely said, "Sorry Jodie."

My face fell. I was in disbelief! Wasn't I the only non-family member to be there anyway? What was the reason for beating around the bush? Besides, there were only four of them so what was one more visitor?? I was being banned for some unknown reason!

Again there was silence. Still trying to absorb his cold words, I turned to pick up my coat and purse and slowly walked out without causing a scene, although on the inside I wanted to defiantly demand what it was I had done wrong. Hadn't I had been good enough to fill the night shift so that they wouldn't have to do it? All of a sudden I could be disposed of like an old shoe! There was nothing I could do but meekly go. It was true. They were the family. I was the outsider. I had no right to insist on being there.

A big lump formed in my throat and I could feel tears welling up in my eyes as I made my way down the hall. Wasn't it just yesterday that I had come down this same hallway in tears, thinking that he had passed away? What was wrong with me? I wasn't used to having my emotions on my shirtsleeves, so to speak. I normally could keep them in check. This man had certainly become a huge part of my life and I didn't even realize the extent until now.

For the second time in a row, I walked in my house with tears streaming down my face as I told Steve the latest. Again he tried to comfort me and reassure me that maybe it was hospital policy and that the family would still try to get me back.

About that time the phone rang. It was Janet. She had received word about her brother in law's illness and wanted to know how bad he was. She was a nurse and certainly understood the gravity of the situation.

She was practically speechless upon learning that I was no longer allowed to see him.

"What must they be thinking? They must have some ulterior motive!" she exclaimed in surprise.

But when she found out what I had told her sister Noreen, outside of Houston's door that afternoon, her comment was, "Oh, no, Jodie. You didn't say that!"

"What was wrong with telling her to check on what type of wound dressing for them to use?" I surprisingly asked.

"Because, knowing how much my sister has to be in control, she would find this suggestion one that was usurping her authority. She would be the one wanting to have discovered this on her own since nursing was her former career!"

"But there was no way she could have known this!" I doubtfully responded. "We wouldn't have known ourselves except through trial and error."

"That wouldn't make any difference," she continued. "And furthermore, your fate was sealed when you told Noreen and Bruce that you brought a preacher in there."

"Why?" I asked in astonishment.

"Because, don't you know that they both are atheists? In fact, I would just bet on it, that you haven't heard the last of her. She will use this against you and your family because I have seen her in action in my own family. She doesn't even need a motive to act vindictively! She will try to destroy you! You are her scapegoat!"

I was so bewildered that I didn't know what to say. Surely, her own sister wouldn't make up those things. I trusted Janet's judgment and felt endeared to her for warning me, but at the same time I just couldn't believe that anyone would be mean enough to go to that extreme. Little did I know!

Janet was planning on being in town a couple days later and wanted me to meet her at the hospital for breakfast. She knew I wouldn't be allowed to get in to see Houston but thought it still might be a good place to get together. Besides, she wanted me to meet Joyce, her one "good" sister. I laughed when she put it that way. We arranged the time and place and I told her I would look forward to it.

Still feeling disturbed about not getting to see Houston, after work the following day I went to the building where he lived, hoping to get a chance to work out plus see some of my friends. I had been getting in the habit of using the exercise room each afternoon before going home. I was thinking that I definitely needed to work out today, relieving some of my stress. I kept my shoes and clothes in his apartment and would change there before going down to the second floor exercise room. The card that gave me access to the parking garage was also the same one I could use to gain access to this room.

I fumbled for the key that Bruce had given me but nothing happened when I put it in the keyhole. Strange. I never had a problem with this lock before. I kept trying but to no avail. I had no idea what was going on but I was about to find out! With determination I marched myself down to security and told Trent, the person in charge that day, about my problem and that I needed to get my workout clothes out of Houston's apartment. He told me someone from the family had just called that morning ordering the locks to be changed because "people" might be trying to get into the apartment to get things that didn't belong to them.

I responded with contempt in my voice, "People! Who else would be going into his apartment but me! I'm the only other person that has a key as far as I know!"

I sure didn't like the malicious insinuation. Trent seemed to understand my predicament and said that as long as he went with me I could get my workout clothes. That way, he said with a mischievous smirk on his face, he would make sure that nothing was taken. He, along with so many others, knew that there was really nothing in Houston's apartment that anyone would want. Everyone in the building had known, from his telling them, how I had brought things in to "redecorate" his sparsely furnished place.

On the way up, people stopped me to ask how he was doing but all I could say was that I really didn't know since I wasn't allowed to visit him anymore but that when I had been there the day before he wasn't doing well at all. Everyone seemed so concerned. I guess they must have wondered why I had the escort of a security guard. But I didn't bother to explain since the whole situation seemed rather bazaar.

Trent unlocked the door and watched while I took my bag out of the closet. I sarcastically asked, "Do you want to look in it first?"

He grinned and declined, then silently I followed him back to the elevator. It hadn't even dawned on me until this point, how I was going to get my other belongings out of his apartment. After his birthday party, just a few weeks before, I had decided to leave my good tablecloth on his table along with some really nice Oriental candleholders given to me by my sister. They were just on loan for a little while so that his apartment wouldn't look too bare after taking down the Christmas decorations. There were numerous other items that I would eventually miss.

I voiced my concern to Trent, who of course couldn't do anything about my retrieval of these items without the consent of the family. I couldn't wait to tell Janet that the first of her predictions were coming true!

The following morning was when I was to meet her for breakfast. The cafeteria seemed congested but I could see her animated face over the crowds of people as she was talking to this other person who turned out to be her "good" sister. As I approached her booth, she jumped up and ran to give me a hug, squealing, "Jodie, Daaaaaling, you've got to meet my dear sister who has heard so much about you!"

I liked Joyce the minute I met her. She wasn't as comical and outgoing as her sister Janet, but she had a heart of gold and was very easy to talk to. How amazing. Here were two special women that weren't even blood relatives of Houston, but in-laws, and yet they were concerned enough to travel from out of town, one out of state, to visit him.

I quickly asked how he was doing but Janet grimly shook her head saying it was still too early to tell if he was going to pull through or not. I was glad he had been alert enough to recognize who they were and knew his spirits would be improved just with their presence.

Janet said, "You'll never guess what happened when we arrived. Bruce took us both aside and lectured us for five minutes saying that we needed to make sure we were out of here before four PM when our sister Noreen was scheduled for her visit. So now it's our turn to be banned!"

"How could he do this to his two favorite aunts, especially knowing that you've come in from out of town?" I asked with surprise written all over my face.

"Because he and his sister are being manipulated by their mother and whatever she says they do. They cower in her presence."

"How sad," I quietly added. "Houston would want the two of you there more than anyone in the whole world, except for maybe his own parents."

"We think that his parents have been banned from coming too!" Joyce offered with a frown on her face.

"No! Now they've gone too far!" I disappointedly said.

"Well," Janet chimed in, "We know that his welfare is not their concern when these decisions are being made. We also believe that Bruce and Elinor are trying to convince themselves that their parents have made peace between themselves."

Joyce nodded with a solemn look on her face.

That made sense to me, knowing how children in divorced families often never lose hope that their parents will get back together. But I knew this belief was certainly far-fetched in their case!

Houston's doctor was a personal friend of Janet's. They had grown up together along with Janet's husband and Houston. She told me she had a chance to talk to him personally that morning and didn't just get a doctor's response. Dr. Radley had reminded her that Houston had been through so much in his lifetime and since he was a fighter, he just might start responding, but on the other hand the situation was indeed very grave. By this time, they had ruled out pneumonia and were suspecting that it was his Multiple Schlorosis kicking in with a vengeance.

Continuing on, Janet told me that she had run into Bruce and Elinor earlier and that both of them said they might join her for breakfast. Since she hadn't told them that I would be there too I knew that this encounter was going to be very interesting to say the least.

I asked Janet if she would do me a favor. Could she please tell Houston that I was thinking about him and that I would have visited him as I had promised but couldn't since only family was allowed. She sadly smiled and said she already had.

"Aunt Janet! Aunt Joyce!"

Our conversation was about to end. Elinor had arrived.

"I'm hungry. Where's the buffet line?"

Joyce pointed the way as Elinor flounced down in the seat beside of her.

"Well, I'll just leave my coat and purse here and I'll be right back."

Her plate was loaded down when she returned. I noticed that she avoided eye contact with me and of course had only spoken to her two aunts when she arrived. When she returned with a tray full of food I quietly observed as she managed to shovel the food in between comments about trivial things.

We heard about the new diet she was going to be trying. She apparently was allergic to most foods and needed to go organic. We heard gossip about some of her co-workers. So and so was filing for divorce. Why was she here if she wasn't aware of how ill her dad was? After about 20 minutes of this kind of talk of little importance, she totally caught me off guard when she turned to me and said with venom in her voice,

"Jodie, I really do need those van keys back right now!"

Startled, now that her attention was directed at me, I slowly started to reach down to get them out of my purse, when out of the corner of my eye I saw Joyce, eyes wide open, vigorously shaking her head and silently forming the word, "NO!"

I immediately straightened up and quickly brought my hand back to my lap. There must have been some reason why Joyce didn't want me to give them to Elinor. I didn't really say that I didn't have the keys. In fact she didn't even give me time to reply. But when she saw me hesitate, she gave me a frosted look and said haughtily, "Well, if you don't have the keys with you, I need you to leave right now to go home and get them!"

Again, Joyce was shaking her head. It dawned on me, why should I go out of my way to do Elinor a favor, when her brother had his own set that she could borrow. It's not like I wanted to keep them for my very own. What would I want with them anyway? But in Bruce's own words just a few days before, he had told me to hang onto his dad's keys in case he got better and I could drive the van there to pick him up. Besides, having to visit another client, I was going the other direction as soon as I was finished with breakfast.

I told her that I really didn't have time to go home (which was true) but that I would be more than glad to give the keys back (I just didn't tell her when). Also, I knew her dad would have had a fit if she had gotten hold of these keys because she had taken advantage of him in the past with her use of the van, never filling it with gas, and leaving it with lots of litter.

She snippily replied, "Well, then, I will just have Bob get them from you sometime in the future."

Fine. That would work out better for me.

Since she now was talking to me, even as uncivilized as it was, I decided to voice a question that had been on all of our minds.

"Has your dad wondered why I haven't come in to see him?"

Elinor looked at me with contempt in her eyes as she replied, "No."

"Have you told him why?" I continued.

"No, because he doesn't need to know," was her answer. "He tells us who he wants to see."

Well, that would have been impossible with his inability to communicate so the question, "How does he let you know?" erupted from my mouth with just a touch of sarcasm.

Janet and Joyce, in the meantime were trying to suppress laughter during these series of questions.

Elinor responded, "After giving him a list of names he lets us know who he wants to see by nodding his head."

Knowing the answer ahead of time but still asking it, I questioned, "Am I on the list?"

"No," she insolently remarked.

My curiosity was satisfied as the three of us witnessed this exchange. For sure, her dad's needs were not the main issue here. We left it at that, as it was beginning to dawn on us that she was playing into her mother's hands. Janet and Joyce explained to me later that there was no reason why Elinor needed the keys so they didn't want me to make things easy for her. I started giggling at the thought of being drawn into "the aunt's" conspiracy against her own niece, thinking, "What harm could that do?"

We finished up our breakfast time and I gave Janet and Joyce a good-bye hug before I left to go to work. They said they would be in town for another day and would keep me informed of any changes with their brother-in-law's condition.

Elinor had already wandered off somewhere so she didn't hear this interchange of dialogue. I'm sure she wasn't too pleased that I was hanging around her favorite aunts but at the same time I couldn't figure out why she was antagonistic towards me.

Later on that day, I felt like I decided to drop by the building to work out, like I had been doing several times a week. Sometimes even my daughter accompanied me and we enjoyed using the equipment together. This time I had my clothes and shoes with me after having retrieved them the day before from the apartment. To my surprise and chagrin, my access card didn't seem to work. I tried and tried again. Still nothing. Puzzled, I rode the elevator down to security to ask if they could figure out what was wrong.

Trent sadly had to tell me it wasn't his choice but "the family" had again called that morning to make sure my card was cancelled.

Wow, they worked fast! I had figured it was a matter of time before they did this but thought they would have other things on their minds to deal with rather than a stray access card to the workout room.

I must have had a blank look as I received this news from Trent. As it registered, I slowly turned and walked out to the parking garage to drive home. They sure covered all the bases. I thought, "Now they've washed their hands completely of me!"

I was wrong again.

The next day when I came home from work I saw that there was a note attached to the front door. Curiously I reached over to read what it said:

Jodie,

You have been warned once and no more. I don't know what kind of game you are playing but you need to give those keys back to me before noon tomorrow or we will be forced to call your employer. Bruce asked me to handle this, so, yes, he is aware I am doing this. He would prefer that you made the arrangement with my husband Bob.

Elinor

I read the note again. Why was she making such a big deal with those keys? It made no sense whatsoever. I hastily turned over the smudged note and saw, ironically that it had been scrawled on the back of a Sunday School paper! Interesting, when she wasn't known to even attend church!

I was at a loss to know her reasoning for demanding these keys back. I hadn't been in contact with her since our breakfast encounter the day before when I recalled her saying I could return them sometime "in the near future" to her husband. I really doubted that Bruce had gotten himself involved with such a petty incident, especially after he had entrusted the keys to myself to begin with.

But I was uneasy about her threatening to let my agency know of the situation. They were unaware of the instability of certain family members and I wasn't sure what other kinds of things she would bring to their attention.

I folded the note and came into the house, thinking I'd better try to reach Bob and let him know when he could get the keys. This whole thing was escalating way out of control. I hadn't intended on it getting this far.

There was no answer when I called so I left a message that I would be more than happy to return them and for him to let me know when a convenient time would be.

Sunday evening the phone rang and it was Bob. He had always been very nice to me and I could tell he felt awkward in making these arrangements. Later on I found out Elinor was using him to do all her "dirty work" and he was just following her orders or else face her wrath.

He asked if I could come down to the apartment to bring the keys and also take out the things that belonged to me. Apparently Trent had contacted them to let them know I still had items I needed back. He said he would be there packing up some of his father-in-law's belongings because they would probably need to release his apartment.

The thought crossed my mind, "How can they make these decisions so soon?" But of course it was not for me to say.

He requested that I meet him at 9 PM, which seemed late to do such a thing, but I guess that's when he planned on being there to work in the apartment. I could have said that the time wasn't convenient but just wanted to get some closure and agreed to meet him then.

I ended up having to pay for parking, since they had cancelled my parking card. I also had trouble getting in the building without an access card. I had to wait until someone left the apartment complex and then I quickly grabbed the door before it closed. I was hoping that being back in his apartment wouldn't be too overwhelming.

I lingered outside his door for a minute before knocking. When Bob answered, he was very polite and accepted the van keys without hesitation, then motioned for me to come in and start packing up. He had a buddy with him who also was helping pack. I didn't notice him at first because I looked Bob in the eye and coolly asked, "Can you tell me what's going on?"

His feet shifted as he nervously glanced at the floor while mumbling, "I don't know. I just do what Elinor says."

In a sense that was true. He sure didn't want to risk her wrath!

Without trying to sound sarcastic, I stated, "Okay, when I'm done you can look in my box to make sure that what I have belongs to me." I certainly didn't want to be accused of taking things that weren't mine!

He quickly exclaimed, "Oh, no! That won't be necessary! I trust you!"

I repeated, "Yes, please, I would feel a lot better if you'd check them."

Again he protested, "No, I trust you."

I had brought an empty box with me but didn't know how I would be able to get everything gathered up in one trip. I didn't want to make more than one since I had parked so far away. Also knowing the building was too hard to get back into was another negative factor.

So I decided to just take the things I knew I would be needing soon like my hand embroidered tablecloth, some of my kitchen utensils I had lent him, along with some of the Christmas decorations. I couldn't bear to take down all the pictures and decorations from the wall. It would have been too symbolic, like saying he was never going to get better. I left those and concentrated more on other things. I tried to avoid looking at the sign I had given him for Christmas, "Forget the dog. Beware of owner!"

I numbly gathered them up as quickly as I could. I pulled my box behind me as I brought it over in front of the door. Bob was in the other room with his friend so I made sure I let them know I was done and still would like for them to look at what I had. Again he refused. I wasn't going to argue but I had this gut feeling that someone needed to check it over or else I would be hearing some accusations in the near future.

I cautiously made my way down to security to have them observe what I was taking. The box was heavy but I kept dragging it behind me as I stepped on the elevator. The timing wasn't the greatest because when I arrived in Security, they were very busy with another problem that cropped up. I didn't have the nerve to ask them to stop and see what I had in my box. Anyway, since I was feeling so wretched, I was sure I would have had a difficult time explaining.

I got back on the elevator and headed up to the lobby, which was the main way out. I was still feeling uneasy about the whole situation. Just as I was getting off, Jamail, our big firefighter friend saw me and asked what was wrong. For one thing he wasn't used to seeing me there at that time, although there had been many times I had come down to answer one of Houston's requests late at night. Also, he must have been able to tell by my face that I wasn't myself.

That evening I saw a new side of Jamail. Even with his massive structure, he was able to show a tender side of him that I never knew existed. He sat me down right there in the lobby and commanded me to fill him in. Between sobs I told him that Houston wasn't any better and in fact was getting worse, that I had been informed I could no longer visit him, and now just the fact that they wanted me to clean out my things and were packing up his belongings, made it kind of a finality in my mind.

Jamail had been around all those years and knew what kind of a bond we had. In fact he had been one of many who had asked why the family hardly ever came around. He lightly reached over with one of his bulky fingers and wiped a tear off my cheek. As simple as this gesture was, it was more powerful than he would imagine.

Later on I thought of how this must have presented an interesting scenario on the security camera downstairs as we were in full view of them. I had no idea at the time, that Jamail was himself going through a difficult crisis where he had just been fired after being falsely accused!

We sat there and talked another ten minutes. Before I got up to leave, I suggested that he should look in the box to see what I had taken from Houston's apartment in case it was ever in question. He casually glanced in it but I could see he was more moved about Houston's condition and concerned that he would feel extremely isolated.

CHAPTER 11

❦

Each day I woke up feeling glum. So much of the challenge had gone out of my day as I realized that Houston certainly had brought zest into my life. I was also missing my many friends that I had made there in his building. I was thankful, though, that I still had my other patients to at least distract me somewhat from his impending crisis. I was hoping they wouldn't notice that the lilt in my voice was gone. After all those years of having such a wide variety of patients, I felt the ones I now had were a "perfect fit" for me.

Arnie and Erma were a joy to be around and appreciated the work I did for them. They were more like family to me.

Mr. Edmore, my newest one and former architect, looked forward to my visits twice a week. Usually I tended to his sore leg and lent a listening ear to all of his tall tales. The combination of his speech eloquently spoken and the eccentricity of his lifestyle made for an interesting visit.

Herman, who had just celebrated his 100th birthday the month before, had been invited to a special event where a local artist had painted his portrait and it was to be unveiled at a local upscale hotel. He had to decline because of poor health but the invitation was such an honor.

I had been with Mrs. Henry almost as long as I had with Arnie and Erma. She was the only client I had on my own and not with my agency. Even though she was in her 90's, she kept up with current events and had plenty to discuss when I arrived for my visit.

That week I found out Skip had been allowed to go visit Houston—very interesting! Bruce even told him, "Feel free to come back anytime."

I was glad for Houston's sake that his old buddy could come in, but on the other hand, he wasn't family and didn't Noreen, Bruce, and Elinor specify that only family could come in? I knew it was all a crock!

My apprehension kept growing though and my heart was heavy to think of Houston being left in the clutches of those that he had such disdain for. I was hoping that his parents would make it down to see him that week as planned. He would definitely have his spirits perk up to have them around.

A few days before they arrived, his mother called and asked if I would do her a favor. Of course I would do anything for her. But when she voiced her request, my heart fell and I knew I would have to tell her the truth. I had been trying to keep his parents from knowing some of the hurtful things that had been happening. I guess I wanted to protect them from feeling the frustration of having their hands tied behind their back. It was going to be Valentine's Day and his mother wanted me to go to the store and buy a red rose on their behalf to take to their son in his room.

When I hesitated, I was sure she must have been wondering why that would be such a hard task to fulfill. I had no choice but to go ahead and tell her the truth, that I had been told not to visit him anymore. Now it was her turn to be quiet.

Breaking the silence, she exclaimed hotly, "Who in their right mind would do such a thing when Houston wants you there!"

"Well, you and I know this, and maybe they do too, but this whole thing is not what your son wants or needs," I added quietly.

"You are so right. I wonder what her motive is, just showing up like that as if she is hovering at his deathbed waiting for him to die so that she can have a piece of whatever he leaves!"

I sure didn't know what her motive was but was remembering from her own sisters that they had told me she didn't even need one. They had been saying all along how she was really caught up with Narcissism.

So it was with a heavy heart that I had to tell Houston's mother that I couldn't honor her request, as much as I would have liked to.

In the meantime, I decided to write a separate letter to both Bruce and Elinor, asking what it was that I did wrong to make them act the way they were towards me now. I voiced my concerns with caution so that they couldn't use the letter as further ammunition. Just as I expected, I never received a reply from either.

❧ ❧ ❧

I had decided that Houston had a "good" side of his family and a "bad" side. Unfortunately, he was powerless and had to be under the spell of this "bad" side. The "good" side still kept in touch and tried to encourage me, saying that they would always be appreciative of all the things I did for him over the years. They knew I had given him a quality of life that he hadn't had for so long. But along with these thoughts, their efforts to help him were ineffective even though they were sure it would have been his desire to have me come back.

Our pastor friend, Ray, placed a call to Bruce but ended up leaving an answering machine message. He asked him to call but he never did. Ray was hoping to find out first hand why I had been banned. I appreciated his support and knew that if Houston found out, his heart would have been warmed to know he had such loyal friends.

Ray had known that my access card had been cancelled and how much I had looked forward to working out each day. One day he called and glibly said, "Jodie, you're getting fat. I have an extra card that you can have so that you can come and use the exercise equipment." He continued, "Besides, about twenty years from now when I need someone to take care of me, you will have your back in shape to lift me in and out of my wheelchair!"

I couldn't believe my ears! I didn't care that he had teased me about getting fat. I was thrilled that I was going to be able to have access to the workout room again!

I had planned to meet with Houston's parents, sister, and brother in law the next day when they were coming from out of town to visit him.

They were going to call when it was a good time to meet and we were possibly going to go out to lunch.

I hung around the house waiting for them to call but they never did. I later found out that his mother had a spell while she was at the hospital and ended up in the Emergency Room herself! I was disappointed from not getting to see them but also was concerned for her. They treated and released her after several hours so the family decided to just go on home. They were worn out from the whole ordeal.

Several dates stand out in my memory. February 5th was the day that Houston was admitted to the hospital. February 10th was the day when the family put him on life support. February 11th was the day I was told not to visit him anymore. And February 20th was another eventful day, again in a negative way.

One day, the scheduler from my agency called and asked me to come by the following day, saying that my supervisor needed to talk to me. I was puzzled because in all my years of working for them, that had never happened. They also gave me an appointment time and again I found that odd.

I was certainly unprepared for what I was about to experience when I arrived. I spoke to several individuals and everything seemed ordinary at first. The receptionist told me to go into the conference room, which I did. I must have waited about ten minutes becoming more puzzled as the minutes ticked away. Just as I was pondering, "What is the meaning of all this?" a group of three women, comprised of my supervisor and two of her co-workers came in. I knew that something serious was about to happen and immediately my smile disappeared.

Their arms were rigidly crossed and scowls were written across their faces as they seated themselves on the other side of the table. I was being scrutinized as they looked at me as if I were the axis of evil!

One of them started mumbling something incoherently. It wasn't long before I realized they were reading off a list of false accusations. I found it all too hard to comprehend and somehow these allegations weren't sinking in.

The one in charge had a thin curved mouth and her eyes darted everywhere except to look at me. Before, we had always been on friendly terms and she had always been very effusive with praise saying I was "one of their best health care workers." How quickly things can change!

After I realized what was happening, my heart felt like it was pounding in my ears and the sounds were drowning out these senseless charges against me. I was shocked! I was speechless! I was numb! I felt as if I were slipping into a bad dream. I was brought back to reality as I heard her say with contempt in her voice, "We take it from your silence that you are guilty of the above, so we need to inform you that as of this moment you no longer work for our agency!"

She continued on with obvious distaste, "and we need to instruct you not to have contact with any of your patients, especially Houston since the family will be putting out a restraining order on you!"

My ears began ringing while their voices started to fade in the background and again, I couldn't seem to find my voice. My thoughts were crowded by suppressed emotions. The situation couldn't have felt more surreal.

I found myself squeaking out some insignificant comment like, "What am I to do with the paperwork from my job at Arnie and Erma's? I worked for them yesterday but didn't have them sign my time slip and paperwork since I was to go back tomorrow."

"Well, we will just have to call them to make sure you were really there and actually did the work!" she replied with disdain.

How quickly I went from having people singing my praises to doubtful comments about my integrity!

Obviously Noreen had persuaded them that they would be better off without me because she could easily sue. They hadn't even checked his file to see that he no longer had a wife, as she claimed to be! Also, Elinor's fingerprints were all over the place as she had been the little snitch to go along with her mother. The two were a coalition.

I had an overwhelming desire to get out of there as quickly as I could. I knew they had already made up their minds before even hearing my side so I wasn't going to waste my time. I emerged from the place feeling defeated and beat down. Was I in the *Twilight Zone*? Was this some sinister plot that I was caught up in? Maybe it was a nightmare and I would later tell Houston with us both getting a good laugh.

I can't remember driving away but I do recall that as I was coming down the hill towards my house, the reality finally kicked in and I said to myself, "They can accuse me unjustly but I won't stand by and let them charge me with one of the offenses!"

One accusation they had made was that the family had told them I had gone out and bought some over the counter cold medicine to give him that fateful morning he was taken to the hospital. That, in and of itself, didn't sound so bad but as they were telling me this, they said giving him this medicine could have masked some more serious symptoms he was having and could have led to his death!

My mind quickly raced back to that last morning when I had noticed a new box of cold medicine on top of his TV but had been too concerned about his cough to ask where it came from.

I decided to immediately call and ask for my supervisor. When she came on the line I told her that I wanted her to know I didn't buy this medicine and that it had been on his TV that morning as I arrived.

"Well, it really doesn't matter," she nonchalantly answered.

"Doesn't matter!" I could hear my voice rising with indignation. "Doesn't matter! How could you say that it's inconsequential when you said it could have led to his death?"

She didn't respond and again I knew she had already made up her mind. For some reason she didn't want to hear what I had to say. Her mind was obviously closed. The matter seemed *non sequitur* to her.

I remember coming in my house in a daze. Enough time had passed now that I could finally try to assimilate what had been told to me. The first thing I did was call Steve at work to inform him what had just transpired. He was astounded. "What were they thinking when they let you go!" he wondered.

They had given three reasons, the first being that I had given out my home phone number to my patients. Yes, they did have a policy discouraging employees from doing that very thing but it was mainly to protect their workers from getting unnecessary calls at home. A lot of my clients had caller ID, including Houston, so that's how most of them would have had my number. I certainly didn't mind that Houston had it. Early on, when I started working for him, Bruce had seen my number on his dad's phone so he programmed it into speed dial. That way, he could call me whenever he needed something.

The second accusation, of course, was the one where they said I made him worse by giving him over the counter medicine.

The third, and last charge was that I had gone into his apartment other than the hours I was given through them. Yes, I was guilty of the last accusation. I remember when I first found out that this was against policy, I had already been giving him extra visits on my own time for over a year. It didn't take me long to decide to continue doing this since there wasn't anyone else going in to help him. I certainly never dreamed it would lead to me losing my job. The thought occurred to me that I might be reprimanded but certainly not fired.

As I finished telling Steve all the reasons for me losing my job he quietly said,

"Hold on. I'll be right home."

He worked only about ten minutes away so it wasn't long before he was there to hear more details. When he walked in the door he somberly stated, "These people are ruthless." He must have been referring to Janet's warning when she had cautioned earlier that her sister's vindictive spirit would rise up and try to destroy our family.

"What do you suppose prompted them to verbally lunge at you?"

"You mean 'whom' not 'what' don't you?" I asked glumly.

I had no answer to give. He asked if I was going to try to defend myself but I told him it was pointless. I had already tried to for one of those points but they wouldn't listen.

So many questions and concerns were floating around in my head. One was, how were we going to make it financially? I had just bought a car two weeks before and had a significant car payment. Another was a question about which one of "The Trio," as Janet had appropriately named them, had done this to me. And it wasn't long before I realized that this meant I couldn't even see my other patients ever again! I wondered what they would do in the meantime. So this was a multiple loss not only for me and my family, but for these other innocent people. I felt wretched!

I wondered how my 100 year old patient would adjust to someone new coming in to help him. These elderly people didn't like change of any kind. His unique situation was a little more challenging than most and not too many health care workers would even want to travel that far under such primitive conditions. I knew his daughter would be dismayed when she heard I wouldn't be coming again. He didn't adjust to new people very well.

Mr. Edmore would get himself all worked up and would make himself sick at the thought of having to get someone new in my place. I had no idea what he would be told but I knew that he wouldn't believe whatever it was.

Arnie and Erma would be thoroughly upset especially after I had been going to their place three days a week for even a longer period of time than Houston. Their grown children would most definitely try to find out why they had to lose me too.

And of course Houston…I grimaced, wondering what he must be thinking right now? What was he being told about my not being there? I knew for a fact that he was thinking that I had dumped him. The first three years I worked for him he used to say, when he was in a serious mood, "Jodie, one of these days you'll leave me in a lurch."

Surprisingly I would ask, "Why are you saying that?"

"Because," he glumly replied, "everyone does."

The last year was the first time he hadn't brought up this concern. He was finally learning he could count on me!

I tried to reassure him that I would never do that. But now there was no question in my mind as to what he must be thinking. I knew without a doubt that he had never been consulted in this major decision.

Holly called that afternoon and after finding out from her dad what had happened, quickly said, "I'm coming over to cook dinner tonight." I certainly didn't feel like making supper so I was touched that she had this way of encouraging us.

Janet found out what had happened and sent me an e-mail,

> Dear Jodie,
>
> Bill and I nearly barfed when we heard what my sister, Noreen, has been up to and when Joyce finds out she will too…eash!"
>
> I don't believe her nerve! I swear she really has gone too far with her game plan-agenda, which she surely has—I'll bet the farm and a bumper crop on it, Jodie. Time will show it all, but she is a smooth operator and I hope that more people such as Houston's parents don't fall victim to her manipulation. She's pretty slick so I'm afraid they might. And actually, if Meganoreen does not get guru-level attention from the people she seeks it from, they are soon dismissed from her life. They seem to have a mind of their own and won't fall for her tactics. As far as Bruce is concerned, he flies under the radar.
>
> Now instead of burying myself in my family's dysfunctional dirt, I'm going to immerse myself in a good book for now.
>
> Love, Janet

I also received a similar letter from Joyce soon after that. She wasn't as "saucy" as Janet but certainly knew how I would be feeling and wanted to convey that she felt bad for me.

> Dear Jodie,
>
> I talked with Janet today and I am so sorry "The Three" are attacking you so viciously. I am not at all surprised at Noreen's behavior, nor am I shocked. She will probably have more surprises for you in her repertoire. I don't know where they will go from here but please know I am (and Janet,

too) in your corner—we just don't know what to do now. We certainly don't want to see you hurt anymore.

Love,

Joyce

A phrase ran through my mind, one I had heard Houston say many times, "The truth will always prevail." But would it in this case? Had someone once said, "Innocence is the greatest defense?"

The next week was a blur. I had no idea what I wanted to do. I knew I needed to apply for a job but didn't know what kind. For sure I wasn't ever going to do this type of work again! I knew I had gotten far too attached to these patients but there was no way I could have done the job without putting my whole heart into their lives. That was just me. If that was wrong, then yes, I was in a line of work not suitable for me!

For the first time in my life I found myself in the unemployment line. As I looked around I was thinking that all the people in there must have stories to tell, but I'm sure their's would pale in comparison to mine. If they heard mine, they would laugh and say I had made it up.

It was utter chaos. No one knew what line to start with so I just guessed.

The first one I stood in was long and hardly moved at all. Twenty minutes later I realized I was in the line for people already established with unemployment benefits! So I moved on to a different line hoping this was the right one.

A stocky lady with an unfriendly face was behind the desk and as she peered over her reading glasses at the next customer, she also showed her annoyance at their innocent questions such as, "How many lines will I need to stand in?" or, "How long is this going to take?"

Fortunately, I got many of my questions answered before my turn or else she would have snarled at me. Why did agencies always hire this kind of person to deal with people? Maybe when they were interviewed for the job they were asked questions such as, "Do you hate people?" or "Do you know how to treat people like scum?"

The next line was a little better but no one could stand in that one until they had completed several pages on the questionnaire. When I came to the question about how I lost my job, I noticed that a comment was added that if a person was fired, one wouldn't automatically get unemployment but the case would need to be evaluated before a decision could be rendered.

I filled the blanks in as honestly as I could, thinking that they would need a lot of time to evaluate my situation especially when they heard from my agency.

There were several more lines to wait in. Then the next step was to create a web site with my resume. I found this task to be the most challenging of all since a resume takes time to put together and has to be customized according to the job description. I started to create one, then saw that they would let me do it at home on my computer within a certain amount of days. That sounded better to me, especially since I had no idea what kinds of goals I wanted to put on mine.

The last station was a room where people were gathering to hear a man give information about what to expect along with all the rules that needed to be followed. After leaving that place, my head was spinning and I really felt like I must be the dumbest person in the world. The information had been so confusing and I had no idea if I would qualify. I naively had thought that The Unemployment Office was there to help you find a job, when in actuality their main purpose was to help get you money for when you are looking for a job. At least I got the ball rolling and maybe I would start receiving unemployment checks in a few weeks. It was a relief to be done with the initial process. Little did I know. There would be many more times that I would have to go back and stand in all those lines again!

I was encouraged to receive many calls that week, mainly from the families of my patients, expressing their concern and sadness about my situation. Arnie and Erma's family were the most upset and were going to immediately quit the agency and try to get me privately. I was endeared to them for their loyalty but told of my reluctance to get myself into a legal situation, knowing that the agency would think that I had taken them away on my own. They assured me that this wasn't the case and I knew that, but again, it would have been a little sticky.

They told me their parents were heartbroken. I told them that I certainly was too. But even though I had been told to stay away from my patients—and that included making calls, I knew I would eventually need to get in touch with them for all of our sakes.

Janet and Joyce, both voiced their sympathy and of course had a hard time suppressing the words, "I told you so," since they had tried to warn me how their sister operated. In retrospect they said, "She's always had an insatiable desire to ruin other peoples' lives." They told me to beware, that she would probably still have some tricks up her sleeve. I didn't think there could be anything else she could do at this point.

Mr. Edmore had never called me before, but he had kept my number from his caller ID in case he ever needed it and this was one of those times. He was almost in tears and said that he had had many health care workers over the years but none that he had felt as close to. I was almost moved to tears myself, and I certainly didn't want to break down over the phone. Besides, I had shed way too many in the past few weeks, more than I had ever done in all my life.

Fortunately he didn't ask too many questions but told me he would always remember me and wanted to keep in touch. I promised that I would and hung up thinking how lucky I was to have had such quality people in my life.

Herman, my 100 year old patient, was unable to call but his daughter phoned me a few days later and said that the agency had told her I had abruptly quit! She knew better than to believe such an accusation. They had sent out someone who had been so gruff and impatient with her dad that he obstinately refused to cooperate. She decided, at this juncture, to put him in an assisted living situation. I thought to myself, "That proves my case, that the magnitude of their deeds didn't just affect me, but had ramifications in other people's lives." How sad that after living in his house all of his life, he would have to leave it now.

Mr. and Mrs. Frederick, (Houston's parents), along with his sister Joan and Tom, got in touch with me. They were all appalled at what had occurred even though they knew Noreen was capable of this very thing and even worse. They reiterated how much they appreciated me going above and beyond the call of duty over the years. They assured me they would always value my friendship. My heart was warmed towards them and I knew that if I had to do it all over, I would definitely have risked my job again!

So now Mrs. Henry was my only patient left since I worked for her on my own. But I only had her one morning a week and that certainly didn't give me enough hours. Many of my friends told me that I was sitting on a gold mine if I chose to take legal action. I was sure that was true but I wasn't the "suing type" and didn't want to stir up any more trouble. Actually, I could have sued "The Trio" along with my agency.

Almost a week passed after that shocking day of losing my job. My phone rang and it was Mr. Richards, the Vice President of the agency that had just fired me. He had been out of town during this ordeal and had just returned that day to find out what had happened. He wanted to hear in my own words what had occurred. Interesting, since my supervisor and her cohorts hadn't bothered to ask.

At first I told him that it would take too long to tell over the phone.

He remarked, "Then we can set up an appointment for you to come over and fill me in."

I really had no desire to run into any of those women who had participated in my termination so I found myself going ahead and telling him what had transpired while he was gone. We ended up talking 45 minutes. He assured me that if he had been around, I would have only been given a reprimand for violating some of the company policies, such as giving out my phone number and going into a home without their knowledge. He had no idea why my supervisor had taken it on herself to fire me over these matters especially since I had never even been given a warning. He was certainly going to sit her down and talk to her.

But he added that, unfortunately, it was out of his hands to hire me back because hiring and firing was in her department. He had also been told by his superior to stay out of it so his hands were tied behind his back. He apologized to me for how I was treated and said he would see to it that I received my unemployment. He also wanted to give me a good reference for wherever I decided to apply since he knew I had been one of their best workers.

Out of curiosity, I asked him, "Can you tell me who started these accusations?"

He quickly answered, "Houston's wife and daughter."

"Houston's wife?" I questioned. "Didn't you know he was divorced?"

None of them did. This bit of information must have been somewhere in the agency's paperwork but they had hundreds of patients with many of their folders being thick like his.

He also said my supervisor had told him I had been taking things from my client's apartment, was taking money "under the table," and was passing myself off as his mistress!

I knew they were going to accuse me of taking things from his apartment after I had felt they had set me up that one night when I went in to get my belongings. I tried to explain to Mr. Richards that Houston didn't even have anything that was worth taking and that the only things I took, belonged to me. But the accusation that I was really appalled with was the last one, of being his mistress??? I almost laughed at that one and reminded him that Houston was a quadrapalegic.

He defended my supervisor for believing Noreen and Elinor because he said that they actually had cases where their workers had set themselves up to "pleasure" some of their elderly patients! To say I was shocked, was an understatement! He went on to say that Elinor had brought in a letter I had written her and used that as some of her proof. I couldn't think, for the life of me, what I had written that would prove I was doing anything inappropriate, but I had a copy of her letter with me and later saw that they must have taken one part out of context. I had said that I *cared* for Houston and would do *anything* for him. I guess they took these two words and distorted their meaning. They certainly wanted to believe the worst!

Mr. Richards, didn't believe it, of course, but questioned why I would write the family rather than come with my concerns to the agency. I reminded him that I had gone to my supervisor on numerous occasions to voice concerns about not receiving my yearly evaluation and promised raise. She kept telling me, "We'll do it next week," or "we'll do it by October." This went on for over a year and I lost all faith in her.

He didn't tell me, but I clearly got the feeling that others in the agency were threatened by Noreen and were afraid that she would sue them. Therefore it would have been much easier to get rid of someone like me, rather than face consequences of her wrath. He seemed just as perturbed as I was and went on to mention he had received letters on my behalf from about fifteen people. I knew Janet had sent them one because she had made me a copy. She had told me ahead of time that she didn't want to share too much about her insane family, for fear that Houston's future care with the agency would be in jeopardy. I understood and told her how much I appreciated her going to bat for me and I was humbled after hearing what she had said.

In the letter she wrote:

> I am writing regarding the termination of one of your employees last week. I am feeling morally and ethically compelled to write on Jodie's behalf, and hope that you might contemplate this case from a deeper perspective than what might have appeared on the surface.
>
> I've known Houston nearly all of my life, and for many years was his sister-in-law. (I am Bruce and Elinor's aunt and their mother's sister.) To say that Houston is special is to minimize his description, for in fact, he is the kind of person one meets, and remembers forever. I have remained, and always will be proud of this humble, creative, adaptable man who has managed to find life and humor no matter how grim his circumstances. It is his good natured personality that has a natural bit of a tease thrown in that makes him such a joy to be around (no matter that he dependently exists in a land somewhere between wheelchair and bedridden).
>
> Houston thinks the absolute world of Jodie and has respectfully appreciated her expert and professional care for these past 3-4 years. At the same time (and you have to know Houston) his personality can't allow any relationship, regardless of how it is 'supposed' to be, to escape the twinkle in his eye and the fun in his words. I've been enduring Houston's friendship and love in this harmless, joyful manner since I was a teenager, and have grown to know that it's his way of having fun each day. As he becomes sicker with his MS, it is his feisty personality and provoking twinkle that

have carried him through. In fact, I believe these traits that are Houston's core have been the glue that has held his courage and dignity together. No one can escape being affected by Houston, not even you folks could, if you were to get to know him, I am absolutely certain!

A year or so ago, on two separate occasions when my mother was hospitalized in Grand Rapids and I flew in from Tucson, I was invited by Houston to stay at his apartment, which I did. During those two separate weeks I was able to observe Jodie come each day, and work with Houston, both providing him outstanding physical care in the most professional manner any agency would want, and tending to his equally important emotional needs as a homebound patient. Every morning she arrived precisely on time, and cheerfully got Houston ready for his day. I would exit from my bathroom ready for the day right about when Jodie would emerge with Houston after the morning hygiene care that she provided for him. Every morning I noted his fresh, clean appearance, his dignity intact (even though a woman had been caring for physical needs that the rest of us would cringe about), and most of all, he emerged from his quarters…smiling and happy. He would sit by his window, drinking the cup of coffee that Jodie had prepared in a manner that left him able to sip it by himself. She did not just dump him there, she made sure that his emotional state was intact, also, and that he was ready for his fairly bleak, lonely day once she left.

For Jodie to not have cared for Houston's complete needs, including his emotional ones, would have demonstrated great insensitivity on her part…something that she is clearly not capable of doing to another human, particularly with this man who makes it a point to subject everyone he meets to his contagious joyful personality. How can anyone find fault with a professional showing compassion and joy with her patient? As an R.N. myself, I can tell you that the mark of a superbly gifted healthcare professional lies in the ability to do the dirty work, and leave the patient in an improved human condition both physically and emotionally.

No doubt, there are others who have come forward on Jodie's behalf besides me. There is not a fiber of Jodie that is underhanded or deceptive, and I wish that her entitled due process had been better served, for if it had, you would have realized that she had no mal-intent for details that were presented to you. To have hung your hats on debatable inferences was your loss in this case, I'm afraid. Whether or not you reconsider your decision to fire Jodie, I believe that it is important to set the record straight as to her professionalism. She is just that, a professional on the highest level, who knows better than most that it is the whole patient who needs to be treated, not just the shell of a man.

I'm not sure whom else Mr. Richards heard from but I do know that Steve felt he should at least give his perspective, so he drafted a letter to the ones who had let me go. His letter read:

> I hope that you will give me an opportunity to share with you some thoughts and feelings about Jodie's recent release from your agency.
>
> Regardless of what you may think about her, I can honestly assure you that Jodie was deeply committed to the well being of each of her clients, including Houston. She was always more than willing to come to his aid, and went beyond the call of duty on numerous occasions as she did with the others as well. Many were the times when she gave serious thought as to how she could make a difference toward their quality of life.
>
> Jodie viewed all her clients with this sense of commitment. Quite frankly, I can only wish that someone like her had been assigned to care for my dad during his last couple of years alive in Pennsylvania. I must confess to you that I am deeply bewildered by her release from Houston, separation from the family, and consequent firing from your agency. From this end, I am at a loss to understand.
>
> If there were issues of performance, I wonder why she was not given reprimand, warning, or corrective directives. If there were inadvertent violations of policy, I wonder why she was not merely given clarification. Further, as an administrator myself, I am concerned that the organization did little or nothing to investigate the allegations brought against her by Houston' former wife and/or the members of the family.
>
> For me, it is a tremendous shame to have Jodie lose her career with your agency knowing how much she poured her heart and soul into it. Again, what baffles me the most is the amount of care and concern she had for Houston and all her clients. I would guess that there are few home health aides with her degree of dedication and commitment, not to mention her wealth of education and experience. Jodie brought great credit to your organization in the eyes of many. Conversely, her release has been a significant disappointment to these and has rendered the organization in a less than favorable light.
>
> Thank you for allowing me the opportunity to open my heart and mind to you.

I did feel a little better after Mr. Richards apology on behalf of the agency but would have rather had it from the ones firing me. I also couldn't understand why they couldn't hire me back. But I guess going back to a company that treated their employees like the way I was dealt with, wouldn't have been prudent. I must have been thinking this would have been the only way to get back the clients I had lost.

One day I stopped by the apartment building to see some of my old friends. Carmen, who worked in the office, motioned for me to come in. Houston and I would always stop by to see her as her bubbly personality would brighten anyone's day. She and her boss, Sally, had been some of the first ones to call and express how sad and disappointed they were with how I had been treated since they had witnessed first hand the good care that I had given their tenant. Carmen seemed almost ready to explode with eagerness to share something that had just occurred in her office.

"You'll never guess who was just here!" she said with a half smile on her face.

"Who," I asked.

"Elinor! She had the nerve to waltz herself in here and act like she owned the place. Frankly, Sally and I didn't even know who she was since she never comes in to see her dad. She immediately started bad-mouthing you saying, 'That Jodie thinks she's a nurse and she's not! My mother is a nurse and I'm so glad that my dad is finally in capable hands.' She even went on to say, 'And contrary to what Jodie thinks, she is not my dad's girlfriend. My parents are in love with each other and are now holding hands since they have made their peace.'"

"Well, that doesn't surprise me. Her aunts warned me that she was going to try to come up with more accusations against me," I quietly said. "Plus I had a feeling she was pushing this parent reunion thing."

"That's not all. She went on to brag, 'Jodie thinks she's the only one who can care for my dad but she's wrong. I've been taking care of him since I was 14 years old so I am the only one who knows his needs.' After she stated that, I wanted to say, 'Then why haven't we ever seen you here in the last five years!' but I didn't!"

Janet immediately wrote,

> ...holding hands? Geeze Louise!!! That makes me throw up and think of what poor Houston would say if he knew she thought this. And of course she would want to say disparaging things about you to make her look good.

I guess the people that mattered, knew the truth. Most people who knew me, would know what to believe. But at the same time, I was finding it hard to hear those false accusations. The task to clear my name seemed monumental. They had certainly cast a slur on my reputation.

So it was with a heavy heart that I headed home to look at the Want Ads. Each day that I searched for a job in the paper, the listings got more pathetic. How would I even know what classification to look under if I didn't even know what I wanted to do? Most were entry-level jobs and I noticed that the same ones were posted every day for weeks to come, probably meaning that no one else wanted them either. I knew that I would be apprehensive no matter what type of job I decided to take. Depression was starting to worm it's way into my life.

CHAPTER 12

I decided to wait to seriously apply for a job after we returned from our trip to Texas. We were going by train to see our son Todd graduate from Basic Training. Our departure was just in a few days. In a sense, the timing was good for this trip, in that I could escape from my unpleasant experience and kind of get a new perspective on my situation.

Pastor Ray called me just before we left, saying he had a great idea. Would I be interested in having him smuggle me in to see Houston when I returned? Would I?? I must admit I got all excited with the prospect of subterfuge and I told him I could hardly wait! Just the thought made me feel endeared toward him.

Holly and Jordan were going with us but our middle son, Drew decided to stay home since he wasn't able to get off from his part time job. He was old enough to be by himself. However he was going to hang out at his best friend's house. He and Justin had been friends since the early years of school.

Holly had ridden a train before and knew what to expect but Jordan was full of excitement as he enthusiastically wrote out a long list of items to pack. "I need to take my Game Boy, paper to draw on, games, snacks…," he said enthusiastically.

"Don't forget to pack your toothbrush and clothes," I reminded him with a smile.

"Oh, Mom!"

At first we had reserved two sleeping coaches, holding two occupants each, but Holly and I decided, after seeing the price difference, that we would be just as comfortable sleeping in the roomy seats that USTram had to offer. Jordan and Steve decided to just stick with the one sleeper.

Steve had planned our itinerary and had so much packed into the six days we were to be gone. We figured that the train trip alone would take about 29 hours one way. The first leg of the trip was from Grand Rapids to Chicago. We had taken this route before and knew what to expect but looked forward to traveling in the bigger train from Chicago.

The day finally arrived for our departure. Drew drove us to the depot and helped load our luggage on the train. I think he seemed a little too eager to leave us and have use of my S.U.V.

We excitedly took our seats across from each other and waited for the train to start moving. We then settled back to enjoy the morning ride to Chicago.

We had scarcely pulled out of Union Station in Chicago when Jordan wanted to see what the rest of the train looked like. We explored each of the cars and made sure we knew where the dining area was. Our ticket included meals and since we had heard how good they were, we were looking forward to our dining experience. We certainly were not disappointed and thoroughly enjoyed what they had to serve us. For dinner we had a choice between prime rib and red snapper. Our food not only was well prepared but the sides that were included made our meal extra special.

We checked out the lounge car where there was a TV and VCR with regularly scheduled movies in the evening. That would be something to do later on.

I suppose the highlight of our trip had to have been the breathtaking nighttime view of the St. Louis Arch. Our train seemed to let us view it from all angles as we passed the structure then made a turn to cross the Mississippi River.

As the train wound it's way through these little towns, we were delighted to see sites that we ordinarily wouldn't see if we had driven ourselves. Later on, when we were going through a small town in Arkansas, we observed a school bus standing on end as someone had made it into a lookout tower. Also, in the same state, we laughed as we saw a car dealership that only had two cars, one belonging to the dealer himself! This was more ammunition for me as I needed to defend my home state!

The gentle rocking of the cars lulled us to sleep that night. Steve and Jordon were cozy in their sleeper car whereas Holly and I had our choice of large spaces to sprawl out in the coach section. The train wasn't full and there were many seats to choose from.

Each of us awoke with anticipation the next morning as the rays from the morning sun crept into our windows. It was nice to lay still and feel the sway of the train cars and hear the clicking of the wheels on the tracks. Others were starting to stir.

Making our way through the dining car for breakfast was a challenge to keep from falling in someone's lap. We still had several hours left in our journey but didn't want to miss anything as we peered out at the sleeping towns we were traveling through.

We passed the time away by playing games while also enjoying the changing scenery all around us. I managed to bring along several books to read and I also caught up on a lot of my correspondence.

Around lunchtime we pulled into the station at the end of our line in Longview Texas. Holly was delighted to be back in the state where she had been born. She had always been teased about being the only native Texan in our whole family but she didn't mind and was proud of her roots.

We rented a car and headed south to Houston where we were going to spend the night with my parents. My brother and his family were there, along with one of my sisters and we had such a nice visit. The time went by much too fast!

We had to get up at four AM to leave for San Antonio since we were unsure how long it would take to get there. We needed to be there by 9AM for an Orientation geared for parents of the graduates. Kathy, Todd's girlfriend, had flown down for this occasion and we were all planning on meeting her before the ceremony began.

We were blown away with the size of the base. It was so big that they had three Burger Kings along with several other restaurants! They even had their own zip code. There also was a mini mall with a food court. Since this was the only Air Force base that held basic training, they graduated 1000 new recruits every week!

Our scheduled orientation was extremely boring. We couldn't figure out why we would have to attend such a meeting. We were told all the things we were and weren't allowed to do while visiting our son and if we did anything wrong he would be recycled, meaning he would have to start boot camp all over again. There were so many ridiculous rules that we were sure we wouldn't ever remember them all. Then we were bussed over to a different part of the base for the outdoor graduation.

We had been told that it would be difficult finding our son since they would all look alike. They were right. He wasn't allowed to come to us but instead had to stand at attention. After the ceremony, all the families ran out on the field to try to find their graduate, which was almost impossible. In fact, we all walked right past Todd at one point. All of them had on their dress blues, had crew cuts, and had their garrison hats on. We were so glad to see him but could only give him a quick hug at the beginning of the visit and at the end since public display of affection was limited.

We were bussed back to the place where we had Orientation and we had a very long walk to his dorm for a special open house for families. We almost got Todd recycled because after we walked over to his bed, his TI (Training Instructor) yelled at him and said we broke a rule by walking down the middle aisle of his dorm. Apparently we hadn't paid close enough attention in Orientation to their silly rules! Todd certainly hadn't exaggerated when he told us how strict they had been treated! As a punishment he was told he would have to do guard duty that night. There really was no rule like that but they just made this one up to show who was in control. We wanted the floor to open up and swallow us at that moment.

We drove around the base as he explained what each building was used for. He wasn't allowed off the premises that day but could leave the following day to see the sites in San Antonio. That evening we stayed in a hotel right beside the base. Holly and Kathy shared a room and we were delighted to see how they had become friends. Before this time they really hadn't had much occasion to spend any time together. They both were the same height and were a size 0 with their favorite activity being shopping.

The next morning Steve drove over to pick up Todd so that he could take a real shower in our hotel before our sightseeing excursion. After a fifteen minute hot shower, he came out all smiles. What luxury after having to endure the 30 second cold showers!

The Alamo was breathtaking along with the sights and sounds of Market Square. One of the highlights of the day was getting to ride on the river boat that wound around through the city. We enjoyed passing quaint little Mexican shops and restaurants. For lunch we ate at a wonderful Tex-Mex place along the Riverwalk and went into some of these shops to look around.

Todd had to be back on base by 6:30 so we made sure we were ready to go by 5:30. He had to be dropped off at the starting point again and wasn't allowed to be driven to his dorm. They were required to walk everywhere and since most places were at least a 15 minute walk, he got a lot of exercise. They also weren't allowed to walk alone so when we drove him back he had to wait until he saw someone that might be heading in the direction of his dorm. This policy was to underscore the importance of the buddy system..

We said our goodbyes and gave him our second hug, the first being when we had arrived. He couldn't come home with us even though he had just graduated because he was to begin Technical School and would be returning home a month later.

Steve had promised Holly that we would make a quick trip over the border but we didn't get to leave until 6:30 that evening. The quick trip turned out to be three hours to Laredo (everyone had told us 1 1/2) so we didn't arrive until 9:30PM.

For days, Jordan had been talking about crossing the Rio Grand and throwing in a plastic bottle that had his name and address on it in

English and Spanish. He was hoping someone would find this bottle and write him some day. But when the time came, as we were walking across the bridge into Mexico, he changed his mind and decided he didn't want to. I didn't want him to be disappointed later on so I grabbed the bottle myself and quickly threw it over the rail. We walked a little farther on the bridge then saw a sign that said anyone caught throwing things over the bridge would be fined $500. Oh, well…too late!

Kathy's prior experience of Mexico had been Cancun so this town was a genuine shocker! We told her that this was the real Mexico! Being a Saturday night, the town was hopping. Music was being played everywhere and the streets and marketplaces were packed with people of all ages wearing brightly colored clothing. We noticed the sidewalks had vast potholes that seemed like they would swallow a person right up and take you down into the sewers.

Steve wanted to eat in one of the restaurants we were passing but we kept telling him that he would get sick. He pointed out one that he tried to get us to go into, saying, "But it would give us a true taste of Mexico."

Holly protested, "Dad, don't you see what's in the window?"

At a closer glance we could actually see several cats that had been sliced open to serve. No thanks! Steve didn't even like live cats!

We passed up our gourmet dining opportunity and continued our brisk walk past all the colorful souvenir stands. We lingered at several as assertive merchants tried to convince us that we needed some of their wares. One brazen storekeeper grabbed Holly's small wrist and fastened a shiny silver bracelet around it. They must have known what they were doing because she ended up buying this piece of jewelry. Each time she tried to take it off, they lowered the price. Finally, she couldn't resist.

We were most amazed to see that there must have been dentist offices on every corner. I spotted a sign that read: "We do Aztec Tattoos and Root canals." I guess they did them at the same time, under the same anesthesia, or maybe even lack thereof.

We would have liked to stay longer but we had a six hour drive back to Houston facing us that night. So we gathered up our purchases and headed across the bridge. We grabbed a few hours of sleep at my parent's house before driving Kathy to the airport to catch a 9AM flight. She wistfully said, "I sure wish I had planned my trip differently. Instead of flying down I should have gone on the train with you!"

She had heard of our pleasant experience and thought it sounded like a lot of fun. But later on, she turned out to be the wise one, in that she had escaped having to go through a "Murphy's Law" trip back!

We spent a nice afternoon with my parents before saying our goodbyes and heading back up north to catch our train. We would have liked to stay longer, only Holly had to get back to her job. That was the whole reason for cramming so many things into such a short time frame.

Unknowingly, our adventures were about to begin. As we were on the outskirts of Houston, and approaching Splendora, Texas, we witnessed an unforgettable occurrence and one we hoped we would never see again. Right there, alongside of the highway in broad daylight, was the Ku Klux Klan trying to flag down cars that were passing by! Most dressed in black were the head honchos but there were also a few white hooded ones waving their Confederate flag. That really should have been an omen of things to come. Wasn't this the very place where that black man was dragged to his death only a year before?

We were quiet for several miles as the reality of what we witnessed sunk in. Jordan questioned what this was all about but our answer wasn't so easy to explain. We tried to give him a lesson on intolerance that our country had yet to eradicate. Our spirits were somber for quite a few miles after that.

We pulled into Longview around 6PM, thankful that we had enough time without feeling rushed. We took notice to a cute little black and white cat licking her paws while she sat on the counter inside the depot. Everyone around us was pointing and calling her the "Depot Kitty." She continued to lick her paw and seemed oblivious to all the attention.

We decided to lug our luggage out near the tracks since the small building wouldn't hold more than ten people at a time. That way we could also be ready to board the train when it arrived.

We first had checked with the agent inside to see approximately where we should stand knowing she would have a better idea where the sleeper car would stop and that way we could get our luggage right on without a hassle.

The temperature had dropped to the low 50's so while we were waiting we were starting to get cold. A half hour passed and when the train didn't come, someone came out and told the ones standing by the tracks that the train was being diverted because of a freight car derailment. We were going to be bussed to Texarkana to catch the train there. This was dismaying news for several reasons, but the main one being that we realized we would have to lug all the luggage back to the front of the depot so that we would be close to where the bus would stop. After waiting another hour out in the cold, the bus finally pulled up for us. Doubts that we would make it to Texarkana in time for the connecting train were going through our minds.

We checked our luggage underneath then quickly piled on to find a seat. The warmth gradually crept through our clothes as we began to thaw out and contemplate what would be ahead. Soon, we were to be suspicious of the driver's ability to actually locate the right depot. After driving for over an hour, he seemed to be taking lots of twists and turns. He actually even completely turned around twice. I'm sure he didn't want to admit that he was lost. We knew he ultimately would find the right place but hoped we wouldn't be too late.

Frankly, we wouldn't have had to be so apprehensive. The train hadn't arrived yet and we still had another 45 minutes to wait when we reached our destination. We remained seated on the bus where we could stay warm and our heads began to nod as the time was just after midnight.

Hearing the train's whistle close to 1AM was a welcome sound. Everyone around us were just as relieved as we were to climb aboard and get our luggage situated. Steve and Jordan got settled in their room while Holly and I found that if we went to the last coach we would have the whole place to ourselves. I guess people didn't want to be bothered to look for more space and had grabbed the first seats available. We were dead tired and knew we wouldn't have much trouble falling asleep.

The last thing I remembered as my eyes closed was that I was thankful we were finally on board, sure that the trip ahead would improve after a good nights sleep.

Breakfast was served until 9AM but we didn't want to awaken until the last minute. So we planned on meeting in the dining car at 8:30. We managed to get up in time but unfortunately there weren't many choices remaining. They had run out of food and only had two servings of eggs and one plate of French toast left. So we split the orders four ways and decided we would make up for it during lunch. But while we were finishing up our breakfast, we overheard two of the servers talking.

One of them mentioned with concern, "Wonder what we are going to do for lunch?"

"I don't know." the other grimly replied. "Too bad we had so many breakdowns coming from California. It was inevitable that with all those delays the passengers would end up eating all the food on board!"

"I've got a great idea." The first one brightly said. "I just discovered some old cans of beef stew in a storage area under the train so maybe we could warm that up and serve it over a bed of rice."

"Do you think they'd go for that after the nice meals we usually serve here?"

"Well it's either that or nothing!"

I couldn't believe my ears! Holly looked at me with concern in her eyes. I knew what she was thinking because she was a vegetarian and that meant she would be eating plain rice. I knew what I'd be eating. Nothing! We had been so spoiled on the trip down and never dreamed that so many problems would crop up on the way back.

Apparently the staff on the train hadn't had a chance to restock their supplies so we would just have to fend for ourselves. Thank goodness for my sister Mary Ann. She had packed up a "goodie bag" for us to enjoy on the trip back. Sure it was mostly junk food but Holly and I especially appreciated having these snacks to get us through.

Steve and Jordan weren't as stubborn and picky as we were so they decided to go ahead and eat what was warmed up for them. Remembering that this was the same husband who wanted to eat at the cat restaurant in Mexico, I thought, "That's not too surprising." I just didn't want to trust the expiration date on the cans of stew.

Our train had been moving along at an average pace. I was immersed in one of the books I had brought along and hadn't noticed that we were gradually going slower and slower. Finally the train cars came to a complete halt in St. Louis after we heard the engine make a loud groaning sound. Unknowingly, we had been pulling 28 freight cars and the load was too much for our engines! That was a common practice among this train line and one that subsidized the cost of operations.

One hour passed, then two, three…When was the replacement engine ever going to arrive? People were getting impatient, demanding to be let off to get something to eat. But that was against company policy. One would have thought that the staff from the train could have called out for food to be brought in.

The replacement engine finally arrived after we had been stalled for five whole hours. The good news was that the engine worked better than the one that broke. The bad news was that it wasn't a very powerful one and reminded us of "The Little Engine that Could." We trudged along at a creeping pace and went even slower up hills, almost coming to a complete stop. Then over the top we picked up a little more speed to make it down to the bottom. Several trains tried to pass us and we had to move over on the side tracks to let them by. At one juncture Holly sarcastically remarked, "That one can't be a USTram train. Look how fast it's going."

My heart went out to one distraught passenger. He was traveling to his brother's funeral and there was no way he was going to make it. I was surprised that the train officials didn't just let him get off to try to make other arrangements.

I skeptically looked at our travel itinerary and knew that there was no way we would ever be able to make our connecting train in Chicago at 5:30. My book had been laid aside long before this time, due to incensed passengers who were pacing the aisles and complaining to everyone who would listen. What a difference from the previous trip going south!

Our growling stomachs told us we needed some decent food. To our delight the steward told us we could have a voucher to buy vending machine food from the snack bar. Several of us chose the Knight Castle hamburgers that could be warmed up in the microwave. I had never tasted these before but had heard lots of jokes about them. On the news only a few days before, there had been a story about some thief who swallowed an expensive diamond from a jewelry store. He had been captured with the thought of how they would go about retrieving this gemstone. Finally the suggestion was made to feed him some Knight Castle hamburgers, which they did, and he threw up the evidence. I tried not to think of this story as I hungrily tore off the cellophane wrapper. I kept myself from trying to remember that we had eaten so much better on our trip down. I guess when a person is hungry one will eat anything.

Finally, we arrived in Chicago at midnight, only 10 hours late! What were they going to do with so many people who had missed their connections? We were herded into a holding room and told that someone would help us eventually. There must have been 50 people needing accommodations for the night and all had missed any kind of possible connections until the next day. Two ticket agents had set up a temporary booth to make necessary changes on our tickets and help with hotel reservations but we had to wait until our names were called. The five hours being stranded in St. Louis should have helped make our three hour wait in the holding room seem shorter but it didn't. People were sprawled out all over the room. Some were sitting on their luggage or leaning against the wall while others were lying on the floor.

After awhile, the four of us got restless and took turns watching our belongings while waiting for our names to be called. The rest of us walked around Union Station.

When our turn finally came we were told that our train wouldn't be leaving until 5:30 PM the following day! We had thought there was also a morning train to Grand Rapids but we had been misinformed. We were going to have to kill time again in Chicago the following day while waiting to get out that evening.

Earlier, Steve and Holly had called their bosses to break the news that they would be a day late getting back to work. Thank goodness for cell phones since we had been unable to get off the train to make these calls. Their bosses weren't very happy but what were we to do?

The train line was putting everyone up in the same hotel and running a shuttle bus to this place only five minutes from the station. They had to wait until the bus was completely filled before they took a group and since we were in the last group, we didn't get to the hotel until after 3AM.

We requested a late check out. That way we didn't have to get up early. We slept as long as they would let us, then checked out and took a taxi over to Union Station to store our luggage in lockers in order to be free to walk around Chicago. We definitely didn't want to be late for the departing train at 5:30 so we made an effort to be back by 4PM. In the meantime, we headed to our favorite pizza place, Gino's, and had a wonderful lunch. Holly hadn't experienced real Chicago pizza before and agreed with us how great it was. Of course our meal was extra good after having vending food and snacks the day before on the train. And what about that canned beef stew!

After retrieving our luggage we meandered over to the area where we eventually would be lining up to board the train. We couldn't see any evidence that a train was even going to Grand Rapids. Puzzled, we inquired at the information booth. The ticket lady was busy shuffling papers while she answered someone's question on the phone. She set the phone down then looked up at Steve.

He hurriedly asked, "Maam, do you know anything about a train going to Grand Rapids?"

"Grand Rapids…Did you say Grand Rapids?"

"Yes," Steve replied.

"Didn't they tell you last night that there is no train to Grand Rapids?" she hurriedly replied. "The track washed out a few days ago and won't be fixed for several more days."

Our hearts sank. What else was going to happen? We had killed a whole day in Chicago just to be told we couldn't take a train that evening? If we had known that, we would have found some other form of transportation that morning. In fact, we decided to do that very thing when they informed us that even though the best they could do was get us as far as Kalamazoo, we would still need to find a way home from there.

Kalamazoo was over an hour from our house. We didn't know how we would get home unless we could get in touch with Drew, who would be at work.

We inquired about renting a car but found out that was virtually impossible without having reservations. It seemed there were no cars available in the whole city.

We tried to call about buses but couldn't get the information we wanted. We were at the railway's mercy and needed to follow through with their suggestion to go on the Kalamazoo train. It didn't seem right that they had neglected to tell us this piece of news the night before.

Eventually we were able to page Drew at work and give him directions to the depot in Kalamazoo. Getting on the train caused another panic because it was at that moment Steve realized he didn't have a ticket for himself! The lady who had made our changes the night before hadn't given it back! We remembered that the conductor didn't take up the tickets until about thirty minutes into the trip and with that in mind, we decided to take a chance and proceed with our boarding. Certainly they wouldn't throw him off.

Breathlessly we climbed aboard the train and tried to get ourselves situated after depositing our luggage in the back of the coach. We found our seats and waited. The train began to move and sure enough, about a half hour later the conductor came around to collect our tickets. Steve began explaining what happened but the conductor looked incredulous. However there wasn't anything he could do but take our word for it and continue on to the next passenger.

We arrived in Kalamazoo around 10:00 and we were so glad to see that Drew had found the depot with our sparse directions we had given him over the phone.

"How was your trip?" he casually asked his sister.

"Don't even go there!" retorted Holly as she gave him her famous glare!

We piled into my Blazer that he had driven and soon we were on our way to Grand Rapids. Our home never looked so good as it did that night. I made up my mind that I wouldn't go on a trip for a very long time after that.

We relived the trip over and over again as we told our story to friends and relatives. There was no need for embellishments to get a laugh! No one seemed to believe that we could have had that many things go wrong. In fact, when I called USTram a few days later, to see about possibly getting some of our money refunded, especially since we had paid for a round trip all the way back home. The ticket agent that I spoke with was laughing so hard that I couldn't understand what he was saying. Finally, when the laughter subsided and he caught his breath, he stated, "Maam, I've worked here for years and I've never heard of those things happening!"

I was glad to provide some amusement for his day. I guess he was ready to give me some humor in exchange because he offered, as an apology, to give us none other than train vouchers for another trip! Now I was ready to laugh and couldn't wait to tell Steve and the family when they returned home.

Our trip had definitely accomplished at least one important goal and that was to provide a diversion to what had happened to me when Noreen caused me to lose so much. I must say that when Steve promised a trip full of excitement he certainly delivered.

CHAPTER 13

❀

One of the first plans that I wanted to do when we returned was get in touch with Pastor Ray, who had promised to smuggle me in to see Houston. My heart beat fast with anticipation as I looked forward to this important event. I wasn't sure how much I wanted to tell him, for fear that he would lose his zest for living but the main thing was to be able to see for myself how he was, restraining order or no restraining order. The whole idea of being hampered by this threat was not going to stop me anymore. More and more I was beginning to realize that "The Trio" didn't have Houston's well-being in mind since their narcissism was so prevalent.

But before I could contact Pastor Ray, Janet called me to warn me saying,

"You'll never guess what they have done to our guy. They checked him out of the hospital, without his own doctor's even knowing, and they moved him to a hospital in Muskegon!"

"What?" I asked with great surprise. "Why would they do such a thing when he had good care here in town?"

"He was going to be put into a Ventilator Unit, but for some reason they wanted him out of town and we both know why, don't we."

Here was another case in point showing that the bottom line was not having the best of care!

Janet had even talked to Dr. Radley who was unaware of what was going on but had expressed surprise especially after knowing that the

Ventilator unit in town still had some spaces available and was known for being the best in the area. She laughingly told me that her husband had recently stated, "Heaven help those people when Houston regains his voice!"

I guess my plans were spoiled. Now, I would have to give this new information some thought before I could arrange my visit to this other hospital. Sure I was disappointed. I couldn't ask Pastor Ray to drive all the way to Muskegan just for a sneak visit but at the same time I wasn't going to be hampered by their latest maneuver.

In the meantime, I kept reading the want ads, making many phone calls, filling out numerous applications but never got any callbacks for jobs. As much as I hated shopping for a reliable car just a month before, this was less enjoyable. I was trying to get back in the field of social work but there didn't seem to be any good prospects. One lead, in particular, turned out to be a real "winner." It was for a Recreational Therapist for a male sex offender program! No thanks!!

I had been determined to stay away from the medical care field. But after hearing such a job description, along with many others that were highly unsuitable, I found myself, against my better judgment, perusing the health care ads.

After pursuing several dead end leads one day, I came home to find an encouraging e-mail from Janet.

> Dear Jodie,
>
> Joyce and I were commenting today how bad we felt that you are having so much trouble getting back into the swing of your career...having it stripped shamelessly from you must make it all feel so, well, completely unwarranted (which it is!).
>
> We heard how Elinor tried to badmouth you to the managers of Houston's apartment. See, Jodie, they are feeling cornered and when people get boxed in, they start to show their true colors. That is what Bruce is doing, (and Elinor's mouth gives her away!) They tried to tell me that YOU were supposed to have caught all of Houston's problems...which was not your "job." They, on the other hand, were supposedly watching Houston like a dutiful hawk (and where was the nurse during all of this?)

It's all completely bogus, Jodie, and everyone knows it. I think even The Trio is feeling squeamy now because they know that it's becoming all way too transparent. (Maybe good will prevail).

Please be assured that we care for you and hope the best will come of this.

Stay strong!

Love,

Janet

When I finished working out one day, I happened to run into Jamail. I had seen him a few times since my trip and had found out that he, too, was job searching for the same reason. A disgruntled employee had maligned his character and caused him to be fired on the spot. We could both empathize with the other so it seemed a logical idea to ask him if he would accompany me to visit Houston. Of course I had to warn him that I had been forbidden to get near him and he would be accused of being my accomplice! His eyes gleamed with mischief when I made the suggestion.

"Sure, Jodie. When would you like to go?"

"Well, maybe we'd both better check our schedules to see when we would have some free time," I said with a smile on my face.

The following afternoon seemed like a good opportunity so I told him I would swing by to pick him up around 1PM. The sun was shining and spring was in the air. Nothing could hamper our little adventure as we both looked forward, with anticipation, to our visit with Houston. Jamail wanted to hear about our trip to Texas. I asked if he had a whole day, but instead I gave him a quick run down. After hearing him laugh, I was sure he must have thought I had exaggerated.

I asked what was on the agenda with his future employment. He told me that he had filed an appeal with the Union and was waiting to hear back from them. Anything could happen at this point. I assured him that all of our friends in the building would be pulling for him.

We eventually arrived in town and tried to find the hospital. The idea of subterfuge seemed to appeal to both of us. After several wrong turns and ending up in a bad part of town, I stopped to ask directions at a convenience store. Before Jamail could tease me, I quickly said, "I'm not lost. I'm just turned around."

He smirked at me and fortunately knew when to keep his mouth shut. We got the correct directions and soon were in the right parking lot. I could hardly wait to see Houston's face.

We were looking for the Ventilator Unit so we stopped at the information booth to find out which floor it was on.

"Second floor, take a right, then a quick left and you'll see the entrance," she impersonally stated to us.

We took the elevator to the second floor and found our way to this specialized section of the hospital. This time we stopped at the nurse's station to find out which room he was in. By now I was full of anticipation as we furtively looked around to make sure we weren't seen by certain people. I knew that he would also be surprised but pleased to see his good friend Jamail. I was sure that he hadn't had many visitors since they had moved him out of town.

We rounded the bend and came to his room, but just before we stepped in, I stopped dead in my tracks. No! It couldn't be! Oh no! There was Elinor herself, parked right by his bed with her back toward us! I could see the movement of her right arm as she was spooning something into her mouth. How could that be when she was supposed to be at work? Janet and Joyce had already called to tell me that no one, that they knew of, had been visiting him since he was so far away.

My heart sank. I knew that there was no way we were going to get to see him that day. (And I certainly didn't want her to see us!) Jamail took my cue and followed me back to the elevator. "What gives?" he asked.

"We couldn't go in because that was his daughter at his bedside," I explained sadly.

"No way! Why would she come all the way here when she never visited him in his apartment?"

"I haven't the foggiest clue," I said ruefully as we glumly rode the elevator downstairs.

Jamail continued to follow me while we walked out to my car. We drove all the way back to Grand Rapids practically in silence. He knew how bad I felt for being deprived of my visit and didn't want to trivialize it with small talk.

I drove him back to his building and thanked him from the bottom of my heart for being willing to help me out.

"Even though our effort was in vain, I will never forget your willingness in going along for moral support, Jamail," I quietly said as he got out.

"Houston means a lot to everyone," he said with feeling, "and I don't like the fact that they are keeping his friends away. Let me know if there is anything I can do."

"You already have."

When Janet found out I had been unable to complete the visit, she wrote,

> Bummer! What a shame that you didn't get to actually go in to visit with him. Come to think of it, Jodie, I'm remembering in Elinor's angry, rude e-mail she sent to Joyce, she mentioned she was off work because of her 'emotional problems' (she was off before for something similar, remember?). I have no idea how long it will be, but my suspicion is that she'll milk it for all it's worth because she very likely gets paid while off work, if it's been medically ordered, which it has. I'm quite sure (based on how well her mouth still works) that she is not ill in any way…she's using the convenience of being off so she can sit in his room rather than her office. (I know her.)
>
> As soon as I find out that she's back at work, I'll let you know. My other hunch is that I'll bet 'The Trio' figured you just might try to slip in there, and I'll bet they've got themselves scheduled to cover the room pretty much most of the time. Might I suggest a late-in-the-evening visit???
>
> Hang in there…this is tough, I know, Jodie. It is just so wrong how this all happened, and it seems even more wrong that they appear to be coming out on top of a terrible thing that they caused…deliberately. You are not alone. There are lots of us who feel this way about the situation.

I did remember that Elinor had obtained an excuse in the past, written by her psychotherapist mother, saying she needed about ten weeks off from work for psychiatric reasons. That meant I probably wouldn't get to sneak in there with her hovering by his bedside.

"You know she won't be there all the time," Joyce encouraged me during a phone call, "She and her mother have a game plan and that's what people do when they get boxed in and feel cornered. They show their true colors." They are placing guards so that you can't possibly get to him."

Something dawned on me. "You know, I just had an idea," I said to her. "She never gets up before noon when she has a day off so maybe I could try to go early in the morning. I know I'll stand a chance of running into Noreen or Bruce but I think that Bruce goes in the evenings or just weekends due to his job."

"That's a great idea," she chimed in. "Go for it girl and you have our blessing. Be sure to tell the old coot to hang in there for us!"

CHAPTER 14

❊

Now was the time to concentrate on procuring a job. No matter where I turned, my eyes kept going back to the medical field in home health care. Finally, I decided to take up the offer from Mr. Richards, my former boss. He had told me he had a good friend who ran another health care agency and would give that person a good reference if I ever decided to go back into that line of work.

"I know you gave 100% of yourself and these people would be happy to have someone of your caliber to work for them," he kindly told me as we finished up our recent conversation.

Reluctantly, and against my better judgment, I gave him a call and told him I thought I was ready to try this new agency. Again, he assured me that these people would be more than happy to have me come on board and he would go ahead and pave the way by calling before I went for an interview.

The scheduled meeting was set up for two days later. I had a feeling of indifference as I drove to this new location. Ordinarily I would have been nervous and desired to impress my interviewers. Not this time. I was still unsure that I really wanted to do this. But I would go ahead into the interview to check out what they had to offer and maybe my outlook on my future would change.

The office was quite small but located in a busy section of town. The receptionist seemed impersonal and hardly looked up as she handed me a battery of tests. I expected similar questions that I had been given four years earlier but instead got handed a page full of Latin abbreviations and what they meant. My two years of Latin in high school was of no avail. Besides, we didn't learn medical terms. Some of these I knew from being around different prescriptions but others left me clueless. Too bad it wasn't multiple choice.

There was A.C. (meaning before meals), AP (apical), NPO (nothing by mouth), P.C. (after meals), P.O. (by mouth), P.R.N. (as necessary), Q.H.S. (every night at bedtime), Q.I.D. (four times daily), T.I.D. (three times daily), plus 30 other abbreviations. I wrote down the ones I knew then guessed at the others knowing I probably was way off target. I was puzzled that this would be a part of the test when my former agency didn't want me dispensing pills, not that all of these were related to pills but many were.

There were several other tests, some using common sense. I had to choose an answer as to what one would do in certain situations such as helping a person walk after suffering a stroke, how one would handle a nosey neighbor asking personal questions about a patient, or listing all the major symptoms of a diabetic. I did better with that one.

My answer sheets were collected and I was told to wait while the receptionist looked them over. Again, I was feeling ambivalent with the whole process. Soon I was called back into an office and this particular receptionist with her rather forceful personality, said in a derogatory way, "You know, it seems you have missed five of the Latin terms and we only allow three wrong answers. You can take the test again if you like but maybe you need to apply for a different type of job. We only hire professionals here."

I must have winced at her disparaging remarks but I'm sure she didn't notice. Somehow working diligently at the other agency didn't count for any kind of experience in her book, not to mention all the years I had worked at a nursing home during the early part of my marriage.

I decided to take the test again after briefly studying the sheet of Latin terms. It would have been nice to have a little preparation before going into the test in the first place. This time I didn't miss any. She took the answer sheet from me and disappeared into the adjoining office where the chief administrator looked it over. Not more than a minute passed when she returned all flustered, saying, "Why didn't you tell me that Mr. Richards recommended you? We don't need these tests in that case because you are an automatic hire." And she proceeded to tear the answer sheets up!

Hearing that I was hired didn't fill me with any feeling of elation. Besides, none of the details such as pay had ever been discussed. Delores, the Administrator's Assistant, called me in her office and was a lot more personable and welcoming.

"We are thrilled that you have come to us so highly recommended. Mr. Richards said that his agency really blew it when they failed to give you the promised raise and yearly evaluation and that it would be their loss and our gain to have you come on deck." Earlier he had told me he wasn't going into detail about how they had let me go.

I told her my reluctance to go back into this kind of work. I didn't go into many details, but did mention that I had just lost a client that I had gotten too attached to. She seemed very understanding and said she was sure that I would be able to handle new cases. However, she really didn't have very many that would fit into my schedule. But being a small agency, she said there was one, in particular, that she was sure I would like.

This began a series of nightmare patients that no one else could get along with! I was the bottom of the pecking order, so to speak, and naturally they would want me to be assigned to the challenging ones. I thought I had made it clear that I didn't want "cleaning" jobs. I have never liked cleaning houses and certainly, if I did, I could get a lot more cases (and money) doing that on my own. Most of the ones assigned to me, ended up being that very thing. My first client was a welfare case that paid to have someone come in several hours a week to help an obese lady. She wasn't sick or old so I was puzzled how she could get this kind of assistance. The most irksome part of my helping her was when I happened to be scrubbing the kitchen floor while she was placing her order over the phone from the Home Shopping Network. Her voice grated on me as she coarsely placed her order over the phone, "I want the 26 inch sterling necklace along with the matching earrings and bracelet."

There was no hesitation in treating me as though I were a hired hand. There certainly was no word of thanks even when I did extra chores to try to please her.

At first, my second client, Mae Rose, seemed very sweet. Again, I was dismayed to find that she wanted me to do three hours of cleaning and very little personal care. But I put up with it, thinking that she, at least, appreciated what I was doing. Although she didn't really have any cleaning supplies, I tried to do my best to improvise. She wanted me to scrub the kitchen floor using a rag, a small coffee can for a bucket, and bleach for the cleaner. Of course there were no gloves to protect my hands.

Her tiny apartment hardly needed one hour of cleaning, much less three, two times a week. Therefore, I tried to think of ways I could use my time more wisely in helping her.

I told her that many of my patients liked me to cook for them. She brightened up and said that would be wonderful and what did I have in mind?

I asked, "What can I make you for supper?"

She thought for a minute then said, "I have a chicken in the freezer that maybe you could thaw out and make some chicken salad."

"Sounds like a good idea," I responded as I headed into the kitchen to get started.

While the chicken was boiling I started cutting up some other ingredients that she instructed me to put in it. By the time I finished making the salad and doing her other chores I had gone over my allotted three hours. But I didn't mind and felt like I had been a help to her. Before I left I told her I would take the chicken carcass out to the dumpster because I didn't want it to smell up her apartment over the weekend. I left feeling pleased that I had finally found something that would be more useful during my time I was to spend with her.

How could one have such a drastic change in personality in just three days? The following Monday I arrived at her apartment, and she answered the door with a snarl on her face. This couldn't be the same sweet little old lady I had worked for the previous week! Her accusation was, "What made you decide to fix me chicken salad? What's wrong with your agency, anyway! Don't they tell you what a person can or can't eat?"

Startled, I responded, "Why, did it make you sick?"

She hesitated then answered, "No, why do you ask?"

"I was just thinking this because of your reaction." I also was remembering that the idea of preparing the chicken salad had been hers, not mine, plus I had made it just like she told me to.

Something told me that I was going to have a hard day. Sure enough, later on I was called into my new office. Delores took me aside and quietly said, "I think we are going to pull you from Mae Rose's case."

Frankly I was relieved but also surprised because with all the challenging cases I had been given with my other agency, there wasn't even one that they had pulled me from and I had around 100 different people. I just stuck with it with the exception of two that I had to walk out on.

I asked Delores what happened and she told me that Mae Rose had been calling them several times with complaints that I refused to do any cleaning for her.

"What!" I exclaimed. "How could she say that when I did extra for her?"

I told her how she made me scrub the floor without any real cleaning supplies. Delores responded, "That shouldn't have happened. We don't expect you to do that kind of cleaning." She went on to say that Mae Rose had told her that I had refused to clean her oven and windows. She hadn't even asked me to—but the oven fell in the category of heavy cleaning and again I wasn't required to do that.

Delores seemed to come to the conclusion that Mae Rose was going through some kind of dementia and thought that maybe if she put another person there for a few days, she would calm down. She ended up having to send three others and the same thing happened. Actually the agency ended up dropping the case.

So, it was with reluctance that I accepted a third person with this agency. Ethel was a constant complainer. It's no wonder her husband wanted someone to come in order to give him a break. She complained when I washed her hair, even swearing at me one day when she said I deliberately whipped the wet ends of her hair in her eyes. I had given her a washcloth to cover them but it still was my fault.

She said I made her break out in "moles" because of the way I scrubbed her back. She was sure I had brought in germs when she came down with the flu. She also had an outbreak of shingles and was positive that I gave her that too. I was at my wits end to know how to please her.

She had me file her nails one day.

"You're doing it the wrong way," she complained.

"Wrong way? What way is wrong?" I challenged.

"Don't they teach you anything? Even an imbecile would know that you can only file in one direction!"

I guess I was a classic imbecile.

I would tell my family that I was going to visit "Pollyanna" and they always knew whom I meant!

Understandably the girls who had come in to help her through other agencies only stayed a few visits and then quit. I don't know why I stuck with her. There were many times that I almost walked out, like the others, but I wasn't a quitter and certainly needed the hours.

For Christmas I liked to bake an assortment of cookies and arrange them neatly on a platter to take to each of my clients. Another gift I liked to give was a book of stamps enclosed in a nice Christmas card. I knew that many of my patients were housebound and usually they were delighted with this gesture.

I visited "Pollyanna" on Christmas Eve but put her plate of cookies on the counter in the kitchen where she would be sure to find it after I left. I propped the card up against the platter, then wished her a Merry Christmas before I left for the day.

Upon my return, she remarked with consternation in her voice, "What was the meaning of those stamps?"

"Meaning of those stamps?" I surprisingly asked in return.

"What was the purpose of those stamps?"

"Oh, I just thought you might like to have some on hand especially since you aren't able to get out and buy any," I lightly reminded her.

"Oh…" and then there gushed a stream of expletives from her mouth.

I grimaced. That had to have been the oddest response I had ever received. Of course there was no thanks or mention of the cookies but I noticed they were all gone. But maybe she threw them away. No. I'm sure she didn't do that. She always had sweets on the counter and they were never anything homemade.

A week later, when I stopped in for my bi-weekly visit, I noticed that there was a pineapple on the counter. I didn't give it a thought but just as I was about to leave she totally surprised me by gruffly saying, "Your Christmas present is on the counter."

I looked around for a Christmas present but all I saw was the pineapple.

"Oh, you mean the pineapple?" I asked

"Yes. I had my son pick it up at the store when he went to get groceries the other day."

I was really touched knowing it wasn't her nature to try to please anyone but herself. Even though the gift of a pineapple was one I had never received before, and was certainly an odd one at that, I felt like we had come a long way. Soon after that she began asking my advice about certain things and even seemed a little more respectful—no, I wouldn't go that far, but at least she wasn't as vocal with her complaints!

CHAPTER 15

A couple of weeks had passed since I had attempted to visit Houston. I still had a lot of breaks in my schedule so I decided to try again. This time I would go early in the morning.

Fog had rolled in during the night but the sun was trying to peak through and it wouldn't be long before the sky was clear. Sure enough, about a half hour into my trip the visibility was improved enough to see a gorgeous blue sky above. Somehow, I knew that this day was going to be special.

This time I didn't have to stop for directions as I made my way to the hospital and then on to second floor. I still proceeded cautiously, though, not knowing if any of "The Trio" would be present. I was certain that Elinor would never have been able to make an early morning visit, so I was safe from seeing her. I was pretty sure that Bruce wouldn't be coming that soon either, due to his new job, where his hours weren't very flexible. So the one I truly needed to watch out for was none other than Noreen, the chief author of this whole drama! Running into her definitely would exacerbate the situation!

My heart beat rapidly with anticipation as I approached the Ventilator wing. I looked over my shoulder while briskly walking past the nurse's station and around the corner to where his room was located. I peered around the door to check to see if the coast was clear before going in. A nurse was busily writing on a chart at the foot of his bed but to my relief there didn't appear to be anyone else around, to my relief.

She turned and saw me hesitating at the door, then promptly left the room to continue with her morning duties. Still nervously glancing over my shoulder, I scurried over to his bedside and looked down on his thin, worn face as the sounds from the ventilator filled up the room. I knew that he would be unable to talk but I was hoping that somehow we would still be able to communicate.

At that moment, his eyes opened…then opened wider…then even wider! The risk of being caught was well worth seeing the astonished look on his face! As I had mentioned before, he was not one to smile, but on this particular day his mouth turned up at the corners as he broke out with the biggest grin I had ever seen. Before this time I don't think I had ever seen his teeth!

All along I had been unsure as to how much of what had been going on behind the scene I was going to share with him. My chief goal was to assure him that I hadn't abandoned him.

I eagerly asked, "Houston, are you surprised to see me?"

He swiftly nodded his head while looking at me with great scrutiny. He was always one to do that, not missing anything, but even more so on this particular day.

"Please forgive me for the way I'm glancing around, but I have to make sure that certain people don't know I'm here. Have you been told why I never came to see you?"

A cloud of sadness came over him as he seemed to be faintly puzzled and he slowly shook his head, "no."

"I'll bet that you thought I abandoned you!" I continued in earnest.

He slowly nodded his head then seemed ashamed that he had come to that conclusion.

"I knew it! I was sure you would think this after you had told me so many people deserted you in the past. But I didn't abandon you! Noreen, Elinor and Bruce have banned me from ever seeing you again!"

I didn't want to go into any details, being unsure as to how the news would affect his physical condition, but he didn't seem to be too surprised with what information I chose to relay to him. I knew from what he had told me about that part of his family, he wouldn't have put anything past them. As the reality of my news sunk in, he looked at me with remorseful eyes.

Dwelling on negative things wasn't something I intended to do, so I moved on to try to encourage him, saying that I brought greetings from all of his neighbors and friends. I told him about my previous visit, when Jamail and I had tried to get in to see him but couldn't. He hung onto every word I said.

Continuing on, I said, "Your parents are still waiting for the right time to try and get down to see you. Of course they have to wait for someone to be able to drive them, and your sister Mary can't get off from school to make the trip just yet. Maybe when the weather clears they will get a chance."

He gaze was penetrating.

"I don't have time to go into detail, but one of these days you've got to hear how our trip on the train went! You'll never believe all the adventures we had," I said with a smile.

I had always felt stimulated with our verbal battles. One would have thought now that our communication would have been one sided but because of all the years and time I had spent with him, we both didn't have any problem knowing what the other felt. His facial expressions said it all.

I wasn't there more than fifteen minutes, the whole time on alert for unexpected visitors. I decided to draw my visit to a close and promised to come again before too long.

I squeezed his hand as I gently reminded him, "Please don't ever think that I would abandon you. I can understand how that must have crossed your mind after not seeing or hearing from me for over a month. I'm not sure when I'll be able to slip back over here since it's so far and I'm back at work again. But I'll try my best to come as soon as I can. Be good and don't give the nurses a hard time."

Again those eyes told me a lot as I left the room. My heart was singing all the way down the elevator and out to the parking lot. I can hardly remember the trip home, except for the fact that I kept reliving those first few moments when he realized who it was that had come in his room. I knew his parents (and Janet) would be delighted that our little plan had worked.

I was a few miles from home when suddenly someone's horn began blaring at me. I was so startled I almost swerved into the other lane but managed to get control before doing so. I kept thinking, "Who would be so rude?" It must have been a few moments before I realized that the horn was MINE!" I was so embarrassed! There was nothing I could do to stop it either! I also noticed several warning lights lit up on my dashboard. Other cars were passing and giving me unkind looks (and gestures). I pretended not to notice and I'm sure they thought, "There goes a dumb blonde!" I remember thinking, "Oh, no, Elinor probably would like to think this was a result of a curse she put on me for visiting her dad after they had gone to so much trouble to keep me away from him!"

The car limped over to the dealership close to our house and after waiting for their diagnosis, I discovered that not only did I have a problem with the electrical system, but my transmission had also gone out! Well, I guess that was my punishment for doing what I did but I certainly wasn't sorry. I had only owned this car for a month but it was a used one. Fortunately, my extended warranty covered the repairs.

So, that was my first bonafide visit with Houston and I silently vowed it wouldn't be the last. Janet was ecstatic that I had succeeded and wrote,

> Your news about the visit was the best news I've had all week! I feel the same as you in that I don't care what 'The Trio' thinks if they find out. The gig is up now that our Houston is on to them (even if they try to pull some more nasties). They certainly will not fool him again. Just keep seeing him, supporting him, loving him and being his best friend, Jodie. Nothing else matters!
>
> I hope Elinor stays out of his face with her wampum feather dust and all because I know he hates that stuff sprinkled around his bed. Yes, it had to have been her voodoo curse on you! If only they knew that you actually defied them under their noses!

A few weeks later I asked my friend Jan to go with me and she was more than happy to be a "partner in crime." We had a mutual friend who had always teased us about being Butch Cassidy and the Sundance Kid. I knew he would be amused after hearing our latest episode.

Jan had met Houston on several occasions and also was impressed with his outlook on life. I knew that he would be glad to see her again and she, him. But before we arranged to go, I decided to call the hospital for an update, and to make sure he was still there. I spoke with a nurse and explained that I had taken care of him through the years and would appreciate hearing an update on his condition. I really didn't get very much information out of her and she seemed almost glad when I gave up and brought the conversation to a close. Later on, after e-mailing Janet about my intentions, she sent this response,

> Dear Jodie,
>
> "Joyce and I were sorry to hear that the staff is being so cautious about answering questions—they are to us, also. They give only generalized, guarded responses (like maybe some {expletive} people have given them orders!!) Anyway (sorry for that little outburst), he is doing better which is all that matters."

Jan and I decided to go the following day, before any more changes were made. We didn't want to be surprised again by finding he had been moved. She met me in town and I greeted her warmly as we began our trip to his hospital. Again, we had to sneak in after looking around to make sure we wouldn't be discovered by certain members of the family. We had a wonderful visit and we also saw how pleased Houston was that we hadn't forgotten him. I could tell he was really bored in his present surrounding. If only he had been left at the previous hospital, most of his friends could have visited him on numerous occasions. He was probably wishing they had never put him on life support.

Jan suppressed a giggle after seeing the colored pictures of animals on his wall. I had told her the story of Noreen ordering everyone to draw these while they were waiting for him to come out of surgery. Joyce had cracked us all up when she recently made the comment, "I'm surprised that Noreen didn't have a picture of herself hanging above his head so that when he came out of surgery, she would be the first thing he would see!"

As bad as his physical condition had been before, it certainly was much worse now. My heart ached to see the pained look on his face while we got ready to depart.

CHAPTER 16

❊

One day after leaving the house of one of my patients, Janet called me. Her calls were always uplifting and invariably we both would end up laughing about one thing or another.

"Jodie, your clients sound like a barrel of laughs…NOT! I'm sure it makes not being with Houston even that much more sour."

She slyly went on to say,

"Guess who I had lunch with today?" She and her husband Bill were vacationing up north at their cottage.

I couldn't imagine.

"Tonya."

Tonya was Bruce's old girlfriend that he had dumped for another friend. I was anxious to hear how she was doing, knowing that she had taken this action with great distress. I also was curious to hear what her feelings were of how Houston was being treated.

"You'll never believe what she told me.," she continued. "She actually had a conversation with Bruce recently and he has her brainwashed. He was harshly criticizing you and somehow she has accepted everything he said as gospel truth. She gave me an exasperated look then said, 'That Jodie has her nerve. Bruce said she did some things that weren't in the best interest of her patient and kept doing actions that he didn't approve of!'|"

I flinched. Why was I constantly having to hear these kind of comments second hand?

Janet went on to say how she tried to defend me but Tonya had already made up her mind that Bruce was telling her the truth and she was closed to hearing the facts. I was saddened that she would believe these lies, after all the years I had known her. In addition, I also was thinking of how Houston and I had comforted her during her difficult days of being rejected. At the time she was reeling from all the ugly things Bruce was saying about her. We had chosen to go ahead and give her unconditional love and not be colored by what was being said. I guess she wouldn't do the same for me. There didn't seem to be any reciprocity these days, not to mention giving people the benefit of the doubt.

Janet was unaware that her revelation would be the last straw for me. I decided to do something I should have done a long time ago—I was going to confront Bruce! Nothing could stop me. I had no idea what I would say but I knew I wanted to find him and ask what it was that I had done to warrant this kind of treatment. He would have to look me in the eye and tell me to my face. I was tired of hearing these things second and third hand.

I wasn't sure where his office was located. He had just quit his job as a disc jockey and had taken a fundraiser job at a business in town. When I got home, I looked up the address then called Steve to tell him what my plans were. He seemed surprised because he knew that I wasn't the confrontational type, mainly because I had seen it done in the wrong spirit. On the other hand he thought that maybe now was the time and the confrontation would do some good.

Determined not to lose my nerve, I hastily drove out to his new office. I was disappointed that the receptionist said he was out on an errand. No problem. I would wait awhile in case he happened to come back. She offered me a chair but I didn't want him to see me in the waiting room and then walk out. It would be better if I would be as inconspicuous as I could until the right moment. There was a table in the corner by the door with brochures so I decided to have my back to him while I pretended to read some of these. In actuality I was contemplating what I would say when he arrived.

The door opened and out of the corner of my eye I could see that it was Bruce. He briskly walked past the receptionist but stopped dead in his tracks when he heard me quietly say, "Bruce."

He tilted his head to look and then turned as white as a sheet. I know he was thinking, "If only the floor could open up…"

I said in a calm voice, "We need to talk. We have some issues to deal with."

He mumbled something like, "Follow me." And I did while he slithered back to his office. He shut the door behind me but began fidgeting, making small talk, and apologizing for the disarray of his office. Actually it did look like a disaster but I wasn't there to inspect.

Finally, he sat down and listened as I calmly but directly stated, "Bruce, I've thought about this for a long time and have decided to come to you in person. I really need to know face to face what it was I did wrong. I am hearing things second hand and don't know what to believe so maybe you can set me straight."

This straightforward talk must have made him very uncomfortable, along with the fact that I was standing and he was seated, because he finally offered me a chair. I knew that Steve must be praying because my thoughts seemed to flow smoothly and I had a perfect calmness. In contrast, Bruce struggled the whole time and never could give me eye contact.

After asking him to tell me what I had done, there was silence for a few moments, then the only thing he could come up with was the following:

"Jodie, you got too personally involved with my dad and it began to interfere with your job."

I bristled then tried not to sigh out of exasperation from hearing this redundant accusation.

"Interfere with my job! What do you mean by that? I need you to give me specifics. No more of these generalities. If you really thought these things, then why didn't you come to me instead of going behind my back and telling people this?" I said as I was trying to keep my voice steady.

His answer really surprised me when he replied, "Frankly, Jodie, I've had a problem with you for a long time."

Again I asked, "Then why didn't you tell me?"

He scowled at the floor as he shifted in his chair, trying to think up an answer. Finally he said, "Because it took several years to be able to put my finger on it."

I had never heard anything so ridiculous in my life but tried to hide my impatience as I wryly reminded him, "Then why did you have me stay with your dad that night in ICU, which, by the way was my last time I was allowed to be with him?"

Certainly this was a mystery if he had had a problem with me for a long time. He didn't have an answer to that question but finally came up with some explanations for getting rid of me after thinking about the question for awhile.

"You asked for reasons. Here are some. First of all you shouldn't have bought over the counter medicine for him. Through the years he has taken this and it's backed up in his system."

I boldly asked, "Are you now blaming me for his Multiple Schlorosis?"

"No, why do you ask?" he replied.

"Because it seems that you have this need to blame someone for the fact that his disease has worsened. It may surprise you to know that my agency allowed me to pick up prescriptions and over the counter medicine for my clients. I didn't administer any of this medicine though since I'm not a nurse." I continued, "I even told my boss that this had been one of the accusations upon my dismissal and he assured me that I didn't lose my job for this reason."

I decided to remind Bruce that he had been the one to ask me to buy over the counter meds for his dad over the years. He didn't deny this fact and even nodded his head as if remembering.

Next, he mentioned, "Elinor told me that you kept changing my dad's wound care treatment."

Frustration and exasperation were feelings that quickly came over me as I heard this latest "wrongdoing!" So now Elinor was the authority on wound care for her father? I kept my agitation under control and had him recall that I took orders from the doctor at the wound care center. I tried to make him recall the times when he had taken his dad for these treatments, long before I came on the scene, and how often the instructions and care had to be changed. That certainly accounted for a whole closet full of dressings, ointments, and other supplies that were no longer being used

"Did you talk to the doctor at the clinic?" I asked.

Of course he had to say no. I could have been coy in mentioning my surprise that he had willingly believed the sister he had no respect for, but I refrained from doing so, He had to have been aware of his sister's lack of involvement in his father's daily care.

Now was the time to play my trump card. With a gleam in my eye I said, "You might find it interesting that not only did the wound care doctor always compliment me on your dad's care when we went in every two to three weeks but he also was one of my references in helping me find a new job." Now I think I really shocked him!

Bruce wasn't about to give up but moved on to another area. It was almost as if I had him cornered and he had to grasp for more offenses to hurl against me.

"Uh, uh...how about the fact that you rallied the troops in trying to turn my family against me!" he stammered.

How pathetic! He couldn't even see that because of his own actions his family sided against him. I tried to gently imply that his family had been in constant contact with me to give me support but I wasn't the one who called them to tattle.

"But didn't you turn Ethel and Jack against me?" His question was almost a whine.

Ethel and Jack were his grandparents and it always irked me that he called them by their first names.

"That isn't true. I tried to be especially careful when I talked to them because I didn't want them to have any more to worry about than they already had. But on February 13, the day before Valentine's Day, your grandmother called to ask me to buy a red rose on her behalf and take it to your dad. Her request put me on the spot so I didn't have any recourse but to tell them why I wasn't allowed to visit him."

Bruce shook his head upon hearing that and said as if he were ashamed,

"Wow, my family is so messed up!"

I didn't question what he meant by this comment but took it that when he used the word "family" he really meant his sister and mother. I think for the first time, he was realizing that they had conned him into believing all those untruths. He had been duped! I guess this was the closest he would ever come to admitting any wrongdoing by blaming them (and of course not taking any of the blame himself!) If this was the way he wanted to rationalize his actions, fine.

I decided to draw my visit to a close, knowing I had had the upper hand the entire time. I ended my confrontation by saying to him in earnest, "Bruce, I know you have had a terrible burden on your shoulder in caring for your dad all these years (I gave him the benefit of a doubt with this comment!) but if you could put yourself in my shoes what would you have done?"

His answer was not surprising. "I have no idea."

Of course he would have no idea! I don't think he had ever thought about my feelings or formidable problem before. He just wanted to obliterate the truth and believe what he wanted to. It was obvious that he cowered under his mother's shadow and became namby-pamby-like.

I thanked him for his time, then boldly stood up and walked out. Maybe I should say that I floated out. I felt great! I was elated! I was liberated! No, I didn't get an apology or even an admission of guilt, but I knew that he finally listened to the truth and he knew that what I told him was accurate. I felt confident I did the right thing in confronting him and there was a certain sense of freedom that I was now feeling—even some sort of closure.

Steve was so glad to hear how our meeting went and before long I was able to call Janet to let her know. She couldn't believe that I had done this, but was so glad that I finally did.

"Jodie, you should have done this long ago," she exclaimed with enthusiasm. "Maybe something good will come out of it, such as his defying his mother and allowing you to visit his dad."

"I don't think he ever would, do you?" I asked skeptically.

"Well, maybe not but he has no excuse now except his own cowardness," she said reproachfully.

So many of us continued to get an update on Houston's condition. Every once in a while he would seem a little better, but then would take two or three steps backwards and we realized that the situation was looking pretty bleak. The nursing staff had been trying to wean him off the ventilator. Some days seemed pretty good then he would have to go back on it for longer periods of time.

About a week later, Houston's mother called to tell me they had planned on coming down to see him because they weren't sure if he would make it through many more days. Their daughter was going to take a day off from teaching in order to bring them down. I was so glad because I knew they hadn't been able to visit him in a while and I was sure that Houston's spirit would certainly be lifted when he saw them.

The phone rang early a few days later. It was Joan, Houston's sister and I could tell by the tone of her voice that she had bad news to share. Our man had lost his battle.

I remember having such a mixture of feelings. I was sad not only for myself but others who had really cared. I was happy that he was finally released from that pain-ridden body of his and that he would no longer have to suffer. I could tell that Joan was experiencing these same feelings and it just helped to be able to talk to someone.

But she was having to deal with some issues. I knew she had planned on bringing her elderly parents down to visit him on Thursday. Having found this out, Noreen took it upon herself to call them, saying there was no need to since he was so much better and that there was no cause for alarm. She even went as far as to say that they had given him three more months to live! Hearing this update, they decided to postpone their visit for a couple more days. That way it would be easier for her to bring her parents on the weekend and not have to take off from work.

But it was the following day (Friday), the day after they would have visited if they had been allowed, that he passed away!

When she told me this I just couldn't imagine how they must have felt! I could tell that she was fighting angry feelings towards Noreen for discouraging them from coming when they had planned to.

She reminded me that the hospital staff had been trying to wean him off the ventilator but when they tried to start him up on it that last time, he kept shaking his head violently. It was then they realized he really didn't want it (and actually never had) so decided to keep it shut off. It was conceivable that he just didn't have the strength to carry on with that kind of life, as limited as it was, and certainly realized by now that the ones who mattered the most were being kept away.

Sadly, Joan told me she would call again when the funeral arrangements were made. I gave her my condolences and told her to tell her parents I would be remembering them.

After hanging up, I remember having a feeling of being cheated. Cheated out of being able to be with him in the end and not having complete closure. And the one who was deprived the most was certainly Houston! Now I definitely was glad I had at least sneaked in those few visits or else I would have been feeling worse. But what about him? I winced thinking of what it would have been like to know he was facing death with those present who couldn't care less, not having with him the ones he cared for the most. He had realized he had been caught up in this sinister plot and he didn't want to be a part of it any more!

I couldn't imagine what kinds of thoughts and feelings were going through his parents heads. I knew they would have a difficult time forgiving Noreen.

My five months of grieving partially paved the way for this day. I wondered about the funeral. Would I be banned from going to that too? Nothing would stop me! I owed it to the ones who really cared and I was hoping we could give each other some comfort.

Janet had just left with her husband on a trip out west so I knew she wouldn't be able to come. I also knew that she would have been here if she could. Joyce planned to come, though, and she asked, "Jodie, how about you sitting with me? My evil sister thinks about as much as me as she does you so we both can be each other's ally."

So it was arranged that I was to meet her in the parking lot at the church, where the funeral was to take place. We planned to walk in together, holding our heads up high.

The obituary came out the following day in the paper. I almost skimmed right past it because they had used a picture that had to have been at least 30 years old and didn't look a thing like him. Several things struck me as being strange in the notice. First of all, when the survivors were listed, they included some of the children of Bob, Elinor's third husband, and these were children that didn't even live with them. I continued reading and almost choked when I came to the part that said, "Bruce and Elinor's mother Noreen who was also Houston's friend…"

He would have been so perturbed that she would be listed in this realm! But that wasn't the strangest part. It was very obvious that Noreen had been the one writing the obituary because after her name she listed her degrees! She actually included, "RN, MSNCS." Several people commented to me how tacky this was. Her sisters said it was a confirmation of her Narcissism.

I shouldn't have been surprised that Noreen had made all the arrangements since the funeral itself was like a circus atmosphere. People were gathered in the foyer, talking in small groups. While I was looking around to see where Houston's parents were, I noticed a small table set up with ten or twelve beanie babies arranged neatly on top. My first thought was that the grandkids had brought something to play with. These toys certainly couldn't be there to symbolize Houston's life because he not only disliked beanie babies, he hated them! I used to tease that I was going to get him one for Christmas or his birthday if he didn't eat his supper or let me put his slippers on. He always rolled his eyes and made some kind of comment such as, "You wouldn't dare!"

Later I found out the reason for the stuffed animals being there. Joyce told me that while growing up Noreen's nickname had been "Beanie." Since the whole funeral really revolved around her, rather than Houston's life, that's why she put them there. She also knew how he detested

Beanie Babies and it was almost like the one last defiant act she could have! Her malevolent deeds never ceased to amaze me!

There were pictures arranged on easels but instead of having the usual ones depicting one's life from childhood until the present, she mostly had ones that included herself. Interestingly enough, she had the wedding pictures, yet they had been divorced for years. I didn't notice but Joyce told me later that Noreen's girlfriend had walked up to these and in a hurtful voice, quietly said, "Oh…my…I never saw these before…oh, dear…"

I made my way over to where the Fredericks were sitting. They were seated in some chairs off to the side. Their eyes lit up when they saw me and I quickly gave them each a hug and told them I had been thinking of them. They told me the same thing and again mentioned how much they appreciated what I had done for their son through the years. No word was said about their being banned from visiting him during his last days and I wasn't about to bring it up!

They called for Jerome to come over to see me. He was Houston's older brother who lived in California. I had met him on various occasions when he came in town to visit and had found out he was a retired Colonel in the Navy. Houston wasn't particularly close to his brother but only seemed to tolerate him when he stopped over. As jovial as Houston's personality was, Jerome's was the complete antithesis. But even though he came across as being staunch and stern, I assured Houston that his brother did care, otherwise he wouldn't bother coming to visit.

On several occasions the three of us went out for coffee. Jerome told me, before I left, that he and his wife were so appreciative of the many efforts I had made through the years to assure that his brother was more comfortable and happy.

I looked around now and saw Noreen and Elinor out of the corner of my eye. Noreen seemed in her glory as she was seeking to be the center of attention. I really didn't want to make eye contact so turned in another direction. There was Bruce standing by his girlfriend, LeAnn. Well, I guess I would go over and talk to him. I wouldn't have been able to do this had I not confronted him a few days earlier. I made my way over and waited for the person who was talking to him to get done. When it was my turn, I hesitated for a second then hugged him and told him I was thinking of him. Of course there was no comment made to me but all he said was, "It's still so hard to believe that he's gone."

"Yes," I agreed quietly, "But I know he's in a better place right now and is free from pain. He wouldn't have wanted to go on living with a ventilator the rest of his life. And to have his speech taken away, that was difficult for him to accept, I'm sure."

LeAnn looked at me suspiciously. I doubt that Bruce had told her about my confrontation with him and she was wondering how I would have the nerve to show my face.

Well, I didn't feel the need to explain my actions and began moving away from them. There was Tonya, Bruce's ex-girlfriend and I suppose, my ex-friend. She glared at me then moved to a different part of the room. Who would have thought that she would turn against me. I knew that funerals bring out the worst in people but her actions had begun before this point in time.

Skip and Martha came. They had certainly been two of his closest friends through the years and I had no doubt they would be there for the service.

Sally, the manager of the apartment building where Houston lived, had come. She came straight over to me and hugged me tightly, whispering in my ear, "I'm sure people here don't realize all that you did for that man. But we in the building do. I know you didn't do it to get patted on the back, and you sure won't get any pats here."

I appreciated her kind words and invited her to sit with Joyce and myself. The three of us went over to view his body in the casket. Somehow I was able to separate my emotions from this action and I didn't have waves of grief coming over me. Again, I was sure it was due to the fact I had already gone through so much of the grieving process before he passed away. Besides, I knew he was more alive now than he ever had been on earth!

I was so thankful for Joyce and Sally's presence. I sat in the middle with one on each side and between the two of them they were more supportive than they would ever know. Actually they brought humor into what would have been a terribly painful experience.

Since Noreen had chosen to have the service in her church with her pastor officiating, there was an impersonal atmosphere that came across as being very formal and boring. Ninety minutes seemed like such a long, long time. Houston's coffin was pushed into the main auditorium and the family members proceeded down the aisle behind it and took their places in the front row.

At one point in the service, Sally leaned over to me and quietly remarked, "Look at all these people who came. Where were they when he was alive?"

She had a point there!

I had prepared a short tribute to Houston, just in case they opened it up for friends and family to give remembrances. I had observed this tradition at other funerals I had recently attended. I certainly would have been tactful and wouldn't have mentioned any of the controversial issues that would have diverted the attention from Houston's life to that of mine. I should have guessed they would have tried to safeguard someone like me attempting to say something they didn't want to hear.

So when the minister announced that only five members of the family were going to speak, my heart sank and I knew I wouldn't get a chance to honor him one last time. All five walked up on the platform, where Bruce began the process of eulogizing his dad. He acted as if he were trying to hold back tears while he began by tritely mentioning, "My father loved the sun. He had many jobs where he was able to spend time outdoors so it seems ironic that the day he chose to die was the first day of summer."

He started to choke up then continued, "If there is an afterlife, I would like to think that Houston woke up on a crisp Fall morning with the sun beating down on his face. In fact, as a tribute to my dad, when I leave this place today, I'm going to shield my eyes and look up into the sun." He paused then lowered his head and left the platform to find a seat near the front of the church.

That was it! How sad. Was that all he could say about his dad when he had so many wonderful qualities? But there really wasn't very many remembrances since he basically didn't have much of a relationship with his dad.

Next was Joan, Houston's sister. She truly was grieving. I felt for her as she groped for words and with a broken voice told how it was like to be a little sister to him. She kept it short then it was her brother Jerome's turn.

He sternly walked over to the microphone as he tried to recall past experiences with his brother. The only one he could come up with was that his brother loved to spout off four letter words. I cringed, thinking, yes, he used four letter words but through the years he had mellowed out and he didn't use them as much. Also, I felt that mentioning this at the service was out of place, especially when he didn't say anything positive. Wasn't there an adage that said, "If one doesn't have anything positive to say about a person, then don't say anything at all?"

I thought he was done but he surprised us by continuing and saying, "and there is someone here today who deserves credit for all the years of care she gave to my brother and without her he wouldn't have lived as long as he did."

All three of us sucked in our breath, thinking, "Wow, he wouldn't dare mention the name Jodie in front of them!"

He went on, "Who am I speaking of? Well it's none other than…Noreen!"

Stab! I think instead of sharpening the knife, they had made it nice and dull so it would hurt more when it went in my back! There went a jab from both Sally and Joyce! Joyce had actually let out an audible gasp at the mention of her sister Noreen and the look of surprise and horror on her face helped me overcome the emotion of the hour.

Jerome turned to Noreen and gave her a smooth hug, as she smugly glanced around and made sure everyone was taking this in. How could he think that! Houston had always said he stayed "out of the loop" with family matters, but I knew he was no dummy and was bound to be aware of what had gone on these last few months. Now it was my turn to punch Joyce's side so she could compose herself and get the shocked look off her face.

By now it was Elinor's turn. The pages crinkled as she unfolded what she had scribbled on several pages of looseleaf notebook paper. A fleeting smile crossed her face while she took a deep breath before reading off all the things she had done for her dad. It was all I could do to keep from laughing. I was so glad not to have to experience her accolades alone. On the third page she read, "and my father just loved it when I came for a visit. His face would light up and he hated it when I left…"

We had to remind ourselves we were supposed to be in mourning and not burst out with fits of laughter! We would have certainly been escorted out if we hadn't been able to contain ourselves.

She continued, "My father was a generous man…"

That was true! I had witnessed his generosity many times as several of his acquaintances called to borrow his van and he never hesitated, even knowing they probably would bring it back without refilling it with gas. I had heard he had loaned a large amount of money, in the past, to some friends then later on forgave the debt.

Anyway, she continued by saying, "My father was a generous man. He loved to help us out all the time."

Again, Joyce poked me. (Sally wasn't aware of how she came in almost every week to take money from her dad.)

She rambled on for two more pages, then turned to her mother and let her wrap up the whole charade.

How well Noreen played the part of a grieving widow. With her children supporting her on either side she stood at the head of the coffin and began listing all the things she had done for her dear husband to make him comfortable during his last days.

It was almost too much to bear. Poor Houston. And he had to endure all of her actions for four endless months!

"And furthermore," she gloated, "Houston and I had the opportunity to go out last week and purchase a bicycle for our grandson's birthday.

We hid clues around his hospital room so that our grandson could figure out where his birthday gift was hidden."

Talk about living in a dream world! Somehow she was trying to make it seem that Houston had not only recovered from a semi-coma but was also able to go out and buy presents! I glanced around and no one in the whole room seemed to question the validity of her statements. Maybe it took awhile for everything to sink in.

The church had prepared a luncheon for those who came to the funeral. Joyce asked if I were staying but I had another commitment, plus didn't feel like I wanted to run into Noreen and Elinor. I had already spoken to the ones that mattered most. Joyce decided that she didn't want to bump into her sister either and decided to leave with me. She had already been given the cold shoulder by Elinor for having the nerve to walk in with me.

As we exited through the side door into the parking lot I turned to her before getting in my car. I told her how much it meant to me to have her be with me during this difficult time. She shook her head and replied, "No, it's the other way around. You have no idea what you mean to the rest of the family. Houston mattered to them and it hurt them to have you taken away when he needed you the most. But we will never forget what you did for him before "The Trio" became involved the last few months. We feel as close to you as if you were part of our family. We've got to keep in touch."

She became teary eyed with that last statement. I was fighting tears myself but didn't want to give way to them. We hugged and promised to e-mail each other. She also said she would be in town in a couple of months and we'd go to lunch. I felt good about that.

I vaguely remember driving to my next commitment. I had another part time job at Ronald McDonald House and had volunteered to help out at a golf outing fund raiser that afternoon. I stopped at home, first, to quickly change my clothes before going out there and when I arrived at the Country Club, went into the main clubhouse to get my assignment, I heard someone say in a surprised voice, "Why…it can't be…Why…it is! Jodie!"

This vaguely familiar person ran over to me and gave me a big hug. Who should it be but a really good friend of Houston and myself! This was Stephanie, who had been one of our favorite waitresses from the café below Houston's apartments. She had left to take another job two years before and we had lost track of her. Unbelievably, this was her first day on the job in the clubhouse restaurant.

"Tell me what that rascal Houston is up to," she mischievously remarked with a smile.

I knew she wouldn't have heard. Where was I to begin? I quietly told her where I had been that very day but before I could get it out, we both were sobbing. Looking back on that day, I really believe it wasn't a coincidence I ran into her at that moment.

Both Janet and Joyce knew I had written a tribute to Houston and they not only wanted a copy for themselves but also encouraged me to send one to his parents, sister, and maybe even Bruce. I wasn't sure about the last one, but decided to run off copies and mail them to the rest. Eventually I did go ahead and send one to Bruce enclosed in a sympathy card. I knew I would never hear from him and I didn't.

What I had written wasn't anything eloquent but was from my heart. I knew just what I was going to write and ended up closing with a statement I had heard him say many times: "I am in great shape for the shape I'm in."

How had I been changed from these past few months? Certainly, I had become more cynical. I had lost most of my naivety and viewed people and situations much differently. After being so thoroughly crushed, I had wanted to protect myself from getting hurt like that ever again. It occurred to me that I tried to keep my distance whenever I began working for a new client.

Some time after this life-crushing occurrence, I heard my pastor ask a rhetorical question, "Have you ever experienced something that was so traumatic? Was this happening a dividing moment in your life or did you use it as a defining period of time?"

My event had most certainly changed me but I didn't want it to be all negative. Someone once said, "Disappointments of the past are necessary for the triumphs of the future."

But I kept wondering what kind of motive or grandiose scheme Noreen had in all of this. Janet and Joyce were constantly telling me she actually needed no motives in doing what she did, but it was their guess that it was a control issue in that it would have to be her and no one else. I didn't fit into the picture and certainly there was a jealousy issue with her not wanting to hear positive things being said about me from others. She could have also thought I was in line to get some of his money, which I didn't even know existed.

Since Houston's passing I had indeed found out he had money. In fact both Bruce and Elinor received an enormous amount from their inheritance. Houston's mother called me one day, very upset, saying, "Our Houston would be upset if only he knew."

"If only he knew what?" I asked.

"If only he knew the final insult that Elinor has done to him."

"What would that be?"

"She kicked Bob out and took Randy, her first husband, back!"

Usually nothing Elinor did shocked me but this about bowled me over! I certainly knew what she meant by the "final insult" since it was Randy that had embezzled money from Houston and now he showed up to get the last of it!

"And furthermore," she continued, "she has lost custody of her kids."

"Who has them?" I surprisingly asked.

"I really don't know. Those poor dears haven't had a normal childhood with her around so maybe it's for the best."

Days went by as I glumly went to work. My heart definitely was not in my job. The patients I now had just didn't "fit." It wasn't that they were obnoxious or difficult, like some that I had been given in the past. Maybe if I would just stop comparing them to the ones I had lost, I would do much better.

One day Janet and Joyce came to town to visit. As we were catching up over lunch, Joyce mentioned, "Jodie, I was thinking the other day that you were sitting on a gold mine. Why don't you write what happened to you and put it in fiction form. No one would ever believe it actually happened since it would read like a soap opera."

I laughed at first at the way she put it, but the more I thought about it, the more this provocative idea appealed to me. Excited at the prospect, I drove home to begin my enormous project. Jordan was extremely helpful in getting me set up on his computer. If nothing else, my writing certainly was therapeutic. In fact there were many evenings I got so involved I lost track of time then all of a sudden remembered I had family responsibilities such as fixing dinner!

Not too long after I got absorbed in this new venture, the phone rang and it was Arnie and Erma's oldest daughter. She began pleading with me about coming back at least two mornings a week since they had just gotten rid of one of the girls who helped out with her parents because all she ever did was eat. I felt that enough time had gone by where my former agency couldn't accuse me of stealing their clients so this time I said, "Yes."

My heart was almost singing as I drove the twenty some miles to their house the following Monday. Arnie greeted me at the door and practically did a song and dance in his excitement to see me! Erma gave me her precious smile and told me how glad she was to have me back after being gone so long. I hugged them both, then sheepishly remembered the vow I had made about not getting too close. Well, maybe I could make an exception this time…

0-595-32145-3

Made in the USA
Monee, IL
22 August 2024